KEYS TO THE CAGES

1930 OHIO PENITENTIARY FIRE

BY

MOLLIE C. CAIN

Prepared for publication by Four Cats Publishing

Cover design by Tonya Foreman

ISBN-10: 0988839938
ISBN-13: 978-0988839939

This book is dedicated to the people inside and outside the prison who gave their time and skills on April 20, 1930, and to the families who claimed the bodies of their loved ones, and to those bodies left unclaimed. May they all rest in peace.

There are some people who are not necessarily good at life.

–Rick Bragg, *Prince of Frogtown*

TABLE OF CONTENTS

Acknowledgments   ix

Chapter 1: 1930 Fire   1

Chapter 2: South Summit Street, Dayton   11

Chapter 3: Children's Asylum   23

Chapter 4: Behind the Walls   31

Chapter 5: Train Ride   39

Chapter 6: Ohio Soldiers and Sailors Orphanage   49

Chapter 7: Sounds of Summer   61

Chapter 8: Commencement   67

Chapter 9: Family Requested Discharges   77

Chapter 10: Newcom Place   85

Chapter 11: October Trial   93

Chapter 12: Kabel Defense   103

Chapter 13: December Verdict   107

Chapter 14: 1917 Train Ride   119

Chapter 15: Ohio State Penitentiary   125

Chapter 16: Prison Life   139

Chapter 17: Warden Ashworth Jackson   149

Chapter 18: Father Albert O'Brien   155

Chapter 19: Black Smoke and Burnt Lungs   165

Chapter 20: WAIU, Reverend Wright   169

Chapter 21: Horticultural Building   175

Chapter 22: Ohio Does Bit   183

Chapter 23: *Columbus Citizen* Ad   185

Chapter 24: Real Accounts   187

ACKNOWLEDGMENTS

I wish to thank Avis and Marcia for their gracious First Reads. I am indebted, also, to Sergeant Ron Re, retired, of the Tipp City, Ohio Police Department for his knowledge of police procedure. I much appreciate the Vandalia and Tipp City Fire Departments, too, for their responses to all my inquiries. Deep gratitude goes to the Diocese of Columbus for use of the many archival papers provided me in my research. Thanks also to the Ohio Historical Society staff. I am further grateful to my husband John and my grandson Calvin for their generosity with technical support.

CHAPTER 1: 1930 FIRE

"Look down upon them, good and gentle Jesus," Captain James prayed, gripped the steering wheel tightly forcing the blood from his knuckles as he pulled out of Number 1 Engine House on Front Street.

"Watch the tanker," complained Fire Chief Sean O'Malley in a raspy voice garnered from a history of smoke-inhaled fires. Chief O'Malley rode shotgun on the open-air engine and twisted his arthritic shoulders the length of the pain they could bear. Water tankers attached to fire engine tailboards rode on narrow gauge tires with thin spindle wheels that easily flipped on turns made by careless drivers. The tanker made the turn, and O'Malley eased himself back into position for the ride to the penitentiary fire call.

The ladder truck followed the Chief's engine. Six firemen stood like a row of corn stalks on the beaver tail. And like blown corn stalks, the men listed left on the ladder truck's hard right turn onto Spring Street. All in various stages of dress, the men displayed balancing skills matching that of a circus aerialist. Alike, each man gripped the rail with one hand. The difference lay in the article of clothing each man wrestled. With a free hand one man jammed his arm into a slicker. Another man balanced on one foot while pulling on his black boot. Two men secured helmet chin straps. The luckier men easily pulled black suspenders up over their shoulders during the open throttle ride.

"Violent fires burn out quickly?" Captain James' tone tried to make his question a statement, but his sideways glance at his Chief revealed eyes that begged an answer. Chief O'Malley sat spine rigid. As an officer, O'Malley was trained to control situations. He controlled even his words and gave James a half-reassuring nod then turned from the pain fermenting in James' eyes. O'Malley's face was emotionless, but the two men held onto the same thought.

Less than twenty-four hours ago, Captain James drove Chief O'Malley down East Broadway in the largest Columbus Easter Parade to date. The brightly polished red engine glided along Broadway in the Easter finery. O'Malley's thoughts turned to his wife who was one of the Easter Sunday Broadway strollers. He smiled remembering an expensive new dress she bought saying it was needed because "hemlines are lower and waistlines are higher this year." Chief didn't know hemlines from waistlines, but when his wife mentioned a straw hat he lifted her straw hat from the top closet shelf and sat it on her head giving her an intimate smile.

"Brimless." Her little finger pointed upwards to the hat. "Brims are in this year, firoghra," she said with the sweet Irish lilt of 'true love' that ended the disagreement as it had ended past disagreements. He was sure it would end all future disagreements because he could not resist her when she spoke in his dearly departed mother's tongue. Every day he looked at her was no different than the first time he laid eyes on the petite lass ewe milking. He kissed her upturned nose, acquiescing he was out of his league. All he ever needed to know about fashion was his chief's uniform.

Captain James turned onto West Spring Street, but Chief never turned to check on the tanker. His thoughts were of the uniformed Knights Templar marching instep leading the fire truck yesterday in the strolling art gallery. Men in raven-black hats appeared to hold up overhead cotton-white clouds while strolling along with their pearl, ivory or gold handled walking canes. The elitist of them donned white evening gloves. Foxes with marble eyes rode along on women's shoulders. A clasp hooked the animal's chin to its tail, making the latest statement of fur fashion of lifeless fur encircling women's shoulders. Easter bonnets about in every color of garden flower. The best-dressed children skipped along beside the fire engine reaching for the candy Chief O'Malley tossed.

"Captain, remember the mother yesterday who sprung along at the side of her son, licking her fingers and pushing down his cowlick repeatedly?" O'Malley's voice scratched the air.

"Yes, Sir." Both men chuckled. "That kid looked wetter than a newly born kitten."

O'Malley cleared his mind of yesterday. Checked his watch. 5:42 p.m. Captain James stopped at the high steel gate and set the brake. The prison wagon gate was locked. "What the hell? Those sons of bitches!" O'Malley had never been in this situation. Locked out of a fire call. Screams of convicts came through the steel bars of the gate as convicts begged. "Let me out! I'm burning!"

O'Malley shifted his mind and mentally started through his checklist: Life Safety - 4,300 population in the path of the fire. Water Supply, man power, apparatus. Static Pressure - 85 pounds. He rubbed his forehead and calculated expected friction loss. Six-inch connectors hooked up to Maple Street's sixteen-inch main. Most of the other hydrants were taken off the six-inch main and a few through an eight-inch that ran back to a twenty-inch on West Spring Street. Hose length, there were several hundred feet of two-and-one-half-inch cotton rubber line hose kept on reels in the yard. "They will be severely tested," he muttered and rubbed the back of his neck pushing a migraine away.

Still they waited. Still men screamed. "This is wholesale death, James, and if I could get hoses between those gate bars, I'd climb the fence and drag them in." O'Malley looked through the bars of the gate. "Fecking useless water!" He screamed at the prison's water tower. "One-hundred, twenty-five-thousand gallons of useless water in that fecking ball of steel. Bedamn water towers."

"Sir, we have a bee that has no honey." Captain James and his Chief knew the tower had no hose connections that they could drain off the water into their hoses. The water tower inside the prison was of no avail to firemen.

"Crow's curse on it. I'd like to shoot the fecking thing. Call for more back up, Captain."

James motioned a runner from the ladder truck waiting behind them. "Dial Box 261."

O'Malley looked at James severely. "We axe down doors. We sit with our thumbs up our arse at a fecking locked gate." A ribbon of flame at the northwest corner of the prison roof licked the night sky. Fanned by the wind, it spread the width of a peacock's tail in various colors of saffron, pumpkin and red. The colors were reflected in the Chief's irises as he looked at James. "Call for a Coroner, Captain."

A National Guard charged the wagon gate, weapon drawn. Looking behind him, he ran forward. O'Malley gripped the top of the windshield and pulled himself to his feet. Narrowing his eyes, he screamed at the cowardly guardsman. "They can't escape! They are burning alive!" Hearing the Chief's words the guardsman snapped to attention and saluted. Chief O'Malley turned a deeper shade of red, "Me bollocks, the fecking turd is saluting. Don't salute me!" The Chief slammed himself breathless back in his seat. "May the devil take your soul." His strong Irish brogue blessed him with the devil. Passing eyeball to eyeball by the man, O'Malley began to cough the acrid, tar-filled smoke. Angrily, O'Malley pushed on the nape of his neck. Ambushed by a migraine, his brain throbbed, his eyes burned and nothing made sense. "I guess when in uniform and in doubt, salute. The dumb bastard."

The guard unlocked the gate. Captain James drove in. Silently, he inched the fire truck into open areas where smoke had undulated upward providing visibility. Never had he seen this display of anger from his Chief. The odor of death permeated the air, his nostrils and his clothing. The sound of screaming men clogged his hearing. His brain wished to be deaf of the screams. He read the Chief's mind a second before the Chief spoke.

"They made a bollocks of it."

"Yes, Sir. They screwed it up."

"No institutional organization for a fire, James . . ." The raspy words broke in the pain of his heart.

"Yes, Chief." James kept his eyes on the blinding smoke he was driving through. He too felt the cause of the Chief's anger. He attended many of the meetings where the Chief asked the Prison Board to institute fire drills and asked them to practice ladder raisings. He even asked the men, maybe trustees, to practice with hand-held extinguishers. O'Malley had preached that reliable trustees trained in fire fighting could be a great asset to the Penitentiary. Some of these men had fought in the war of '18. They were already trained in fire fighting. All the Chief was given were these words: "The prison is fire proof."

James snaked his way through National Guardsmen, city police, state police and Fort Hayes soldiers under the raining screams of scalding men. "Jesus, save me!" People were running. He revved his engine to roar his presence maybe in warning of the runners, maybe to drown out the screams. "I am burning! Dear God save me!" The smoke waved around him the way his mother's sheets waved on the clothesline. The odor of death that had permeated his nostrils he could now taste.

"Call for a third back up!" O'Malley ordered. Flakes of falling ashes caught in his hair as he rode into prisoners' anguished cries. What he had heard from a distance at the gate now up close sliced his heart the length of a razor leaving scars that never heal because those scars reopen with every memory never allowing the forming of a scab that holds the pain back.

"Fire proof. Gobshite. The Prison's doxology was that the Penitentiary is built of stone and brick. The concrete ground floor leaves no chance of fire." Captain James nodded his head to the Board's words concurring in what they overtold the Chief.

He remembered at a Board Meeting the Chief asked, "What about the cell bunks, mattresses, blankets? What about the four folding wooden chairs in the two-man cells, overcrowded that now hold four? What about the wooden table in each cell and the two wood shelves connected to the back cell wall? You've seen those shelves that you so proudly say were built to hold prisoner personal letters and family pictures? You know to help rehabilitation. All combustible!"

He remembered how none of the Board looked up at his pleading Chief. They kept their heads lowered, and they pushed puny papers around on the table in front of them while the Chief stared them down in silence. Had they raised their eyes they would have seen his Irish temper. How many meetings had he cautioned an inside first line of defense would save lives? How many times did they have the power to prevent this crematory?

"I promise you are being fool hardy," Chief O'Malley warned.

The Columbus Dispatch published minutes of Prison Board meetings. Never did the minutes include the Chief's pleading speeches. Articles succinctly stated, they met with the Fire Chief, leaving readers to interpret all was right with the world. Judges kept on sentencing, and the walls kept on bulging.

"Captain James, call a fourth alarm." A runner cranked the call box at 6:03 p.m. The scene was organized chaos with firemen dropping off engines and running with hoseline to hydrants along the south and west outside walls. Dennison Avenue supplied the most hydrants, three. Maple Street had a hydrant outside the north wall. No hydrants stood inside the gray prison walls. Thirteen pumpers and five truck companies with approximately one-hundred-and-forty firemen arrived on the scene. The number of men became considerably higher as off-duty men arrived.

Surrounding the yard, slivers of moonbeams danced on metal-gray Tommy guns positioned in the four corners of the thirty-five-foot stone walls. Each machine gun straddled a tripod, and each tripod chaperoned the unblinking weapon that was trained on the yard.

Slate-colored uniformed prison guards perched along the prison walls between the machine guns looked not unlike crows on telegraph wires. On the ground below, muted inky shadows of men emerged from the smoky haze. Dressed in ashy gray, prison pants shirts and caps, the worker ants carried charred bodies to mouse-colored blankets. The convicts deposited the remains among lumps of blanketed, grotesque bodies. One convict knelt beside a lump who he was told was his brother. Gently he lifted the blanket's corner. Charred skin adhered to the wool and with the blanket came the man's face. Was it his brother?

"Gangway. Comin' through!" A convict shouted, brushing past O'Malley who stood beside the fire engine. The convict's clothes were laced in vomit froth. A group of convicts pushing wheelbarrows of blankets divided around O'Malley formed again and went on to dump their load in the prison courtyard. These were the men from the lower cells who got released. Fires burn up, but this fire was on top, on the roof, and it was burning downward. O'Malley saw prisoners helping firemen carry hoses that would not reach the top cell floors.

"Shit." A convict stepped on a spongy corpse forcing air from a dead body that sounded like the snore of a sleeping man. O'Malley turned to see the frightened man prance away in steps of a cat carrying a newly caught field mouse. The man pranced across the courtyard until he reached the solid, cement sidewalk.

O'Malley shouted orders through his megaphone in a yard void of color. Gray smoke covered gray dressed men as he moved among the chaos forcing his voice to be heard above the sounds of screaming men. "I'm burning! Let me out!" O'Malley watched his men aiming their hose water toward the top of Blocks I and K. All around men were drawing near their barred windows, having given up on their locked cell doors being key opened. "Shoot me!" they screamed. Flames first singed their hair then blistered their skin. Noxious gases felled crazed, caged men who stood at their windows and called, "Mama!"

Chief O'Malley never had this many people burning in an apartment building. Even the large apartment on Neil Avenue, and he thought maybe the incinerating men were looking into the face of the mothers they were joining in heaven. He leaned over and vomited just to clear the awful taste in his mouth.

"The men carrying men out say they are putting wet towels on their back that have steamed deep blisters on their skin, while they died with their heads in toilet water. Men are cutting cellmates' throats then applying shivs to their own throats." Captain James told his Chief and went back to his duties.

O'Malley thought about the murders and suicides all mixed up under the collapsed roofs as he watched the eyes of his men and thought to himself, these were once little boys who played fireman, policeman and soldiers. They grew up believing they could save lives. Now they helplessly watch human pyres. Tears sprung from his Irish eyes, from pain not smoke, and for the first time he knew it would be his last fire. "What the hell?" The water stopped spraying. O'Malley ran to a policeman and screamed. "They are parking on my hoses. They've cut the water."

The cop ran to the gate and peered through. Outside the walls, citizens collected faster than bees on honeycomb. "Jesus, Mary and Joseph, they are parked on the hoses, impervious of their deeds."

A state patrolman passed him. "I've ordered men to disperse the gridlock. We know they are blocking fire apparatus, medics and clerics." Gawking people stared through the gate bars into the face of the ashen-white city policeman. "Clear the streets!" shouted the state patrolman. "We will shoot you if you don't get your cars off fire hoses!" It had little effect. No one moved until Fort Hayes soldiers marched double time out the gate.

"Fix bayonets. Prick them into obedience," the Master-Sergeant called. The crowd grabbed children and headed for their cars.

Outside the prison walls, strolling the perimeter, the rifle-toting Warden offered his explanation to a blue-suited reporter who wore a Press Card in the band of his hat, who asked him a question unheard by the crowd. The Warden gave his reply, loudly for all to hear. "Smoke exacerbates my asthma. I can't go in there. But I'll shoot any escapees out here."

Families turned wooden radio knobs and tuned into Firestone Theater. When instead they heard the painful shrieks of dying men in its place they fiddled with the dial thinking they were on the wrong station. When they realized it was a live broadcast, the men ordered their wives out of the room and children to bed. People were horrified and yet like a boxing match draws blood and a broken-legged racehorse, the radio mesmerized listeners who simply could not turn away.

~ ~ ~ ~ ~ ~

Across town at the Neil House Hotel, Dick Fidler's

Orchestra rehearsed for the night's ballroom entertainment. Then, Robert Derringer made last-minute changes in his presentation for the Ohio Federation of Women's Clubs' week-long convention.

Danny, a young hotel employee, struggled with a table leg. "Hey, did you guys see how orange the sky is tonight?"

Drummer Hank laid his cigarette on the ashtray lip, hit a few beats, twirled his sticks in the air, caught them and asked. "Danny Boy, you talking sunset?"

Danny shrugged his shoulders. Sweat dripped onto the stubborn leg he wrestled. "Yea. Kinda. I guess," he said as he glanced out the window. The Columbus Neil House previously burned to the ground, twice. Both times Hank narrowly saved himself. Not his drums. Tim, Alto-Sax, saved himself and his horn on both of those occasions. Piano player, Ken, eyed Hank. They read each other's thoughts and moved to the windows. Over West Spring Street, a mysterious umber-colored sky glowed against the darkening sky.

CHAPTER 2: SOUTH SUMMIT STREET, DAYTON

Papa tousled my Irish ginger curls. "Let's take a walk, Theo." He extended his gnarled hand. Papa entered the Great War with fingers straight as straw but exited with lumpy, arthritic nodules due to years of "starless nights bedded on ground that leeched my bones of calcium and deposited mean ole' gout mixed with rheumatism," he said. His eyes grew lifeless on many occasion and became hardened glass as he said, "Many a night he told us he slept on soil that held more water than could be squeezed from Mama's dish rag."

"When did you get those dimples?" Papa asked looking down on my plump, tight-skinned baby hand.

"The Archangel's kisses." Proudly I recited my Mama's teachings, "Michael, Raphael, Urial and Gabriel."

"Why would angels want to kiss Theo Kabel?"

I giggled. "Papa, you know they send all babies out of Baby Land with a kiss on each hand."

"Papa, tell Theo how he was sent to another family who refused such an ugly baby. Tell him how the stork slipped him under Mama's covers and by the time she discovered him, the stork had flown away and we were stuck with no way to return him to Baby Land." James Junior, who paired up with our other brother Puddin Head behind us, taunted.

James Junior got his name before my parents knew he would be the spitting image of his namesake. He was as tall as Papa and carried the same brown hair, with the same front cowlick. He was just as impatient as Papa. Both possessed hair-trigger tempers.

Puddin Head was like Mama's side. Short, squat and easygoing, like a round blob, Puddin was just as bland as vanilla. Eventually, 'Head' fell off and

11

everyone just called him Puddin. His Christian name, George, was after our maternal grandfather who was killed in the Great War. But his Christian name never replaced Puddin.

Papa winked at me. His smile widened, "Theo is just right for our family." Our foursome stepped out on a heat-shimmering sidewalk, delivered by a cloudless May sky as we headed to town. At the southwest corner of Third and Main Streets, we thankfully entered the dabble shade offered by the awnings of the Philips House, a grand ole dame who ruled the rich and famous by demanding formal dress for dinner and unallowing visitors in the upstairs rooms. The cost of this code of conduct: rooms are four dollars a night. No visitors are permitted to loiter in the hallways beyond the first floor dining room. 'ALL GUESTS MUST ENTERTAIN VISITORS IN THE LOBBY.' So the sign read. With one exception, President and Mrs. Lincoln.

"President and Mrs. Lincoln overnighted at Philips House," Papa exclaimed, his eyes darting at the traffic as we stepped off the curb. I strained my neck in a backward arch, sliding my curls off my shoulders and down my back trying to catch a glimpse of any rich and famous person standing framed in the purple, velvet-curtained windows. None appeared. Papa held my hand and led me around buggy wheels taller than my four years of growth. We halted for horse carts and dodged overloaded hay wagons that moved past me like a mountain in motion, blocking out the sun. Finally we reached the northwest corner and Papa finished his thought. "That was eighteen and fifty-nine, when the Lincolns visited Dayton."

We caught our breath on the corner where the bourgeoisie are ruled in a miniature Parthenon standing atop a great mound of dirt in an eight-foot wall corset of Dayton limestone. The elevation of Dayton's courthouse is an affirmation of the building's importance.

Papa displayed the seriousness of one approaching an altar. He might have even dipped a knee. His eyes watered in the unhurried way snow melts as he spoke, "President Lincoln delivered his speech from these courthouse steps. And I marched off to the Great War from this corner under the notes of the Civil War Band. Over there," he pointed, "stood a public board where telegraph messengers wrote names of men killed or missing. And sons, if a street sweeper could have swept all the names written on that board into a pile, the pile would have traveled around this walled courthouse three times and stood three times as high."

My brothers and I stood in respectful quietude, while Papa's thoughts dwelled on his War. When his moment passed with a slathering of damp memories the length of his shirt sleeve we turned and walked west on Third Street. Directly behind the courthouse, the Sheriff's home fronted Third Street. The pearl gray two-story Hansel and Gretel house, dripping of filigree, was poles apart from what one would expect of a gun-toting Sheriff's residence. A half-moon staircase delivers a visitor to the front door then bends back down to meet the sidewalk. Like a sitting cat's tail, the jail juts straight out the back of the Sheriff's home. Jail birds amuse themselves caterwauling at passersby seamlessly.

"Mister, wanna sell that kid?"

James Junior plucked me off the ground, lifted me up on his shoulder and asked, "How much?"

"A penny."

"Sold! Ouch!" he yelled as I grabbed a handful of his hair.

"Put me down." My bottom lip pouted out and my eyes filled with tears. I was horrified and so afraid of those bodiless, prisoner catcalls and whistles. "Papa!" I screamed sliding off James Junior's shoulder. Papa scolded my brother. When my feet hit the ground, my pout dissolved with the sight ahead. On my left, down the length of Wilkinson Street tall elms sparred with the sun and according to the number of sunshine pools on the sidewalk veneer, the sun won. There cordoned behind a tall boxwood fence, the Boy's Academy stood majestically against the azure sky. I knew all about 'The Academy'. Mama said it demanded perfection in everything. "Theo, the boys march in silence through the halls when they change classes. The Academy uses the Zaner Bloser method." I nodded agreeing, but having no idea what upper and lower case meant. Guarded by two topiaries, and Mama's promise, my entrance to an academic future lay before my eyes.

Mama taught us as best she could. Reading our letters sprang from her *McGuffey Primer*. Noah Webster's *American Speller* meted our lessons. Our sums and subtractions were introduced by *Ray's New Intellectual Arithmetic*. As Mama taught me, " A-Rat-In-The-House-May-Eat-The-Ice-Cream." The total of hornbooks, plus our Bible, eclipsed the number of books found in neighbors' houses by three, Mama said. Headmaster Barney assured Mama I would be accepted next year when I became five years of age. I held fast to that promise. "I'll be back," I whispered passing the Academy.

Approaching us was a tall, gaunt, white-haired man under a long, soot-black stovepipe hat. Wrapped in a tailored black coat, all but his prominent nose and deep-set eyes, which had been marked by crow's feet live hidden behind a hoary white eiderdown beard. The beard floated to his waist and there decided to give up lengthening. The man carried a wrinkled black leather bag that had been perforated by two bullet holes. "Good Morning, Dr. Clark." Papa fingered the brim of his hat, a tribute to a fellow veteran. I watched the eiderdown shake gently as a feather rode a wind current. The doctor's downward eyes did not meet Papa's.

"Dr. Clark's hair turned white in the length of the

Chickamauga Battle. Townfolk have branded him an odd duck. He walks behind funeral processions carrying a large sign with big, black letters, 'This was not my patient'." James Junior snickered and Papa knuckled his head faster than a rattlesnake strikes. Puddin laughed, but then his face sobered quick enough not to be cuffed by Papa. "Do not question the workings of another man's mind," Papa was beet red, "Specially a man that has lived in the trenches of war, you buggers!"

~ ~ ~ ~ ~ ~

Protesting squeals of a passel of pigs could be heard but not seen until they rounded the corner of Maple and Third Street, being coerced into a semblance of obedience by a black-and-white, blue-eyed Border Collie. Devoted to his drover, the dog pushed the pigs with complete submission to his master's whistled commands. "Noah could have used that dog on the Ark," Papa cleared his throat.

"I bet that dog could herd a school of minnows." James Junior laughed watching the dog nip at the pig's hand legs but never touched their skin. "Remember our pig?" James Junior peppered Puddin with back slaps. "That old sow snatched Theo out of Mama's laundry basket like it was gonna suckle him."

"Or eat her young." Puddin interjected.

"She carried Theo the length of the backyard, him swinging from his dydee. Mama screaming and chasing that sow all the time repulsing clothespins off her broad, humped back, until the sow dropped him." James Junior laughed tears.

"Didn't you see me open the back gate?" Puddin wheezed. "The pig and Theo could have both been rendered into soap."

"Yep, but I took up log-beating that sow because Theo was having too much fun."

They continued laughing over the incident that made me the butt of their joke. Too young to remember, I held my mouth in a hard line and quickened my steps ahead of the group. Aromas of freshly baked goods drifted from an open door, and I inhaled deeply sucking the smell down to my empty stomach. The smell of raw skins and acid mixed together and rose out of tanner's vats and assaulted me in a musky, vinegar stench. Mama's sister, Aunt Liza, fell in a vat, and the tanner pulled her out and married her two years later. Uncle Simon said he had to wait two years for the smell to die away. Sacred Heart's bell tolled away the laughter I left behind.

Sacred Heart Church was built on the west side of town as a rite-of-confession to the overcrowded of east side, Saint Joseph's Church on Second Street. Sacred Heart's domes are framed in our formal parlor's window and serve as a backdrop for Mama's tradition of 'Tea Time'. I guess because Mama has no daughters, she invites me for tea. Setting out her English bone china, Mama pours the walnut-brown liquid into her lilac, hand-painted cup. While it steams, she fills my cup of painted violets with sugared milk and finishes it off with a splash of tea. Our time was sacred. Mama and I sipped and watched buttery sunbeams plunge down the vast middle dome of Sacred Heart, while bullet-like beams ricocheted off the two smaller domes placed obliquely on either side of the church front door.

We reached the western pastoral edge of town and entered the bridge spanning the Great Miami River that cradled our city gently in the curve of its arm three seasons a year. Then as promised by the native inhabitants, the river angrily rose out of its banks in the fourth season. Spring floods twisted newly planted crops around planter's cabins, indiscriminately, and washed both down past Hamilton and down the Mississippi River, tumbling everything into tiny pieces until Ohio homes and crops became delta silt.

A lacy ironwork train trestle lay over the river on our left side. Children stood on the narrow track of the bridge until an oncoming train set track into earthquake-like vibrations. The first child to jump was labeled 'Chicken'. Children drowned jumping into the river below, resulting in our parent's forbidding us to play on the trestle. My brothers played on the track, and one day when my nerve was bigger than my brain, I tagged behind my older brothers at what I felt was a safe distance, until James Junior jumped out of a bush. His temper flashed sharper and brighter than heat lightning, and he pummeled me until Puddin pulled him off. "I promise I will toss you from those tracks into the mouth of a giant catfish and watch you sucked beneath the river's surface, if you ever tell Papa!"

Since that day, I gave the ice-bedded catfish at the Main Street Market House a wide berth. Once I noticed the fish in the vendor's case follow me with his eyes, and then it happened, a fierce catfish's mouth moved as I passed by the glass front case. I was walking behind Mama toting her market basket, and I threw it down and fled the market without a word to her. Outside I stood shaking, and people asked me if I was lost until Mama came. I told her I just could not stand the smell of the market and I thought I was going to be sick. Ever after she let me wait outside.

"Ouch!" James Junior knuckled the back of my skull. He must have read my thoughts. Papa glared at my outburst. "Rock in my shoe." I lied putting a limp in my step as the four of us rounded the corner at Summit Street. Temptation loomed for me under the canopied tree-lined avenue.

"Temptation comes in many colors," Mama claimed. My seducer stood outstretched before me darker than a black bat night. The workings of the devil brought my heretofore good behavior down. I chose a fallen oak limb and went to work raking the sturdy rungs of the front yard fences perched on a tiny, rounded cement curb. The wrought iron ran an unbroken city block, and the cacophony of my endeavors lifted a bevy of black birds from favorite roosts in such quantity they darkened the sky. Dogs on porches howled until rolled newspapers slapped their backs and sent them yelping under overcrowded, wicker porch furniture. Raised hands of grown men shook their fists at me as I ran long the fence line.

"Gobshite," Papa yanked my oak limb and flung it backwards over his shoulder into the street. The limb barely missed Sergeant Dayhoff who rode on his police patrol wagon. Sergeant's big-hoofed Morgan pushed the oak branch deep into the street mud. I watched it disappear in a wet, sounding slurp. My brothers froze, wide-eyed and open-mouthed at Papa's faux pas. Quickly, he saluted Dayhoff who gave us a smile in the same manner Father Osterday smiled down on miscreant children at Mass, carrying a message for parents to control their children.

Collectively, we turned our back on the paddy wagon and entered a gateless gap in the fence line. Our entrance chopped off Papa's morning conversation leaving us in silence that was louder than our flagstone footfalls. We threaded our way along a daffodil-lined walkway as daffodils nodded to our knees. Short, trumpeted narcissus swayed in the air currents of our passing. Hidden under the tall flowers' slender leaves were bunches of ripe, purple grape Hyacinths. We walked up the path two by two, just the width of a parent and child.

Oh, how I longed for Mama to be with us. The perfectly manicured lawn was lined in lilac trees, and Mama said, "When you see a lilac tree, Theo, count the heart-shaped leaves. That number is the number of heart beats I hold for you."

Mama's dressing table held a cut glass atomizer the purple such as only God paints rainbows. The months on the kitchen calendar measure nothing for Mama.

She is interested in one season and that is spring. Spring is the duration of lilacs adorning her sideboard. Mama irons lilacs and presses them into the fold of her handkerchiefs and nightgowns. Her highboy is lined with lilacs melting a sweet aroma into her clothing. Compassionately, Mama places lilac-oiled cloths against my earaches as she rocks me. When white-hot summer sun shrivels lilac blooms into bunches of hard, round green seed pods, Mama's spirit shrivels a bit as she plucks the seeds sorrowfully in the manner she plucks goose feathers, never wanting to hurt the bird. So tenderly she removes the seed pods. Mama's spirit sinks losing something I feel but cannot name.

Christmas past, my brothers bought Mama a cloche, and our neighbor Mrs. Headapohl gave them a violet to put under the bell-shaped glass. I hoped the purple violet would thrive in the little cloche and carry Mama until spring brought back her lilacs. It did not work. By Valentine's Day, the leaves turned an ugly brown and dropped away. "Things die from too much care," Papa declared and threw the plant on top of the backyard garbage pit. I set the plant off to the side and replaced the glass cloche with an old jar. No one spoke of the oncoming violet buds. Then one morning, I saw the jar was gone, nowhere to be found. The morning frost had shriveled the plant and rendered a final death to the recovering violet.

"Papa, I wish Mama was here." He ruffled my curls but did not reply. The flagstone path dead-ended at a stern looking, three-storied building pinned to the sky by six chimneys. A stingy front porch contrapositive to my generous porch at home. Our porch was furniture filled, and it beckoned friends to stay long and laugh loud, according to Mama. This porch we stepped up on offered a heavy windowless door. We crossed it in five scant steps. A doorman caught Papa's undelivered knock in midair. Papa dropped my hand, and I moved behind his leg. Single file, ducks in a row, we followed Papa.

The foyer rested under a four-sided cupola. Slice sunbeams rained through the glass above. It showered our shoe tops. The shards of sunlight did nothing to warm the stark room that lacked conversation chairs or soft hassocks. The no-nonsense foyer contained a cold, hard mahogany table centered with an oil lamp. The space demanded callers get on about their business. Off the foyer was a room with a large paperless desk. Behind the desk sat a sour-faced matron who wore a high starched collar rubbed in the back by a severe bun. Heavy glasses performed a balancing act on the end of her Roman arched nose. She frightened me more than Sergeant Dayhoff, and I moved behind Papa's leg and grasped hold of his pants. "Christ's Little Ones." I sounded out the cross-stitched words framed on the wall behind the matron. Her huge bosoms rose over the edge of her desk, and she plunged toward me. Landing half way across the desktop, she barked.

"Little ones are to be seen not heard."

I ducked my head behind Papa and nestled my face into the back of his pant's leg. It was something I did not understand. Fire burned his eyes into the matron. With one hand he reached around and patted the top of my head. And it was still longer before he spoke, "We are very proud of Theo's ability to read." My heart stopped in mid-beat. My breathing ceased. Papa never praised something he was lacking. I gulped down a sob wishing Mama heard. My fingers dug into the flesh of his leg.

"Names?" The matron levied against Papa pulling herself backwards and dropping her bosoms out of sight. The gesture pulled her goiter neck back inside her starched collar. Papa's gaze searched her face. He was not willing to let her go with the insult to his blood. He weighed the battle. His decision was made and he offered her.

"Kabel, James Junior, George and . . ."

She gave him a nose-clearing snort. Papa's tongue stuck to the roof of his mouth in a silent 'T', Theophilus as the woman lifted a metal handbell and clanged it wildly above her head.

Curse her, I thought and shouted, "Theophilus Kabel!" Papa reached behind his leg and boxed my ear. Tears welled in my eyes and flowed over my cheeks. My heart called for Mama to be here and now.

A large walrus-moustached man appeared. Sprouts of dandelion fluff hung out his ears and nose. His nametag matched the dour matron's desk plate. "Follow me," he snapped his fingers in the air exposing gold cuff links.

My brothers joined him. I stood firmly gripping Papa's leg until he splayed his fingers across my back and sent me stumbling forward. I pitched on Puddin and regained my balance and then turned back to Papa. A windstorm of dust mites whirled where he had stood. He was gone.

CHAPTER 3: CHILDREN'S ASYLUM

"Older boys upstairs." Walrus adjusted his ascot, while James Junior and Puddin peeled off to the right, taking the stairs two steps at a time. I took a following step. "Not you." Walrus clucked his tongue and drove his manicured fingernails deep into my shoulder. I felt hooked and hung like meat in a slaughterhouse as he moved the length of the hall. I opened my mouth to scream a protest, but my voice took flight from his evil stare.

Walrus pushed me into a small room, slammed the door and shoved me toward a black leather chair too tall for me to climb. He yanked me off my feet, raised me up and slammed me down on a knotty pine board which lay across the chair's arms. The sound of my landing was a ricocheting smack of wood. "Harold!" Walrus pirouetted, hollered and exited leaving me precariously balanced and shaking uncontrollably and gulping down silent sobs. My butt stung with the pain of a hundred mud daubers.

The soft noise of sloughed off covers came from behind a dirty draped curtain that cut off a corner of the room. A loud belch followed an acrid fart. Harold threw aside the curtain and exposed a stained army cot encircled by squat, empty gallon glass jugs. I wiped my watery eyes. A man with red-rimmed eyes and a hard lined mouth stepped from behind the curtain. The hairs on his face and neck stood in pus-filled pores, on skin the color of a July Fourth sunset. "Barber's Itch." Papa called it, saying he knew men in camp who caught it during the Great War and itched themselves into a grave in a shorter time than a bullet would find them.

Harold grabbed at the air near me. My pretend resolve poured down my face in tears of terror. Harold curled back his lip over his four remaining tea-colored teeth. His hand caught a side hanging strap on my chair, and he raised a gleaming straight razor over my head just to hear me scream. He laughed cruelly. His laugh was in the gentlest of whispers, and goose bumps rose on my arms. Frantically, he slapped the razor to the leather. "Chin on your chest." I remained stone hard, unsure of what he meant. Harold never repeated himself. He folded my neck over like a foraging swan and cut off my breath then he worked me over shouting, "Oops." I struggled with sips of breath. Blood trickled from his oops.

Papa expected my curls to be shorn on my first birthday, as was the case with my brothers. Mama said second birthday. My third birthday came and went unnoticed. My fourth birth year arrived with my curls intact and Papa exploded.

"Hell's fire, Anna! The lad is four! Stop making a sissy out of him and stop the damn tea parties. Cut off his curls!"

Indolently, Mama tilted her chin up to him. "Do not swear in my presence, Mr. Kabel." Her cream-softened pallor could not have been more opposite Papa's angry, red color. She had never defied him in front of her children. "Theo's curls are God's gift to me and me alone. You know I will never be blessed with a daughter." She leaned into him. "And Mr. Kabel, I shall make a hair bracelet of those ginger locks when and where I see fit to cut Theo's hair." Her voice remained steady. Her intent plain and her freckled nose punctuated her words to the man glaring down on her.

The man glaring down at Mama however was never willing to let a quarrel drop. So he changed strategy to keep their open fight flowing in front of my brothers and me. "You talk to God more than I called on Him during the height of battle." Mama's back was rigid under the accusation, knowing Papa was jealous of her devoutness to the Lord. Papa longed to be first in her heart. He was the youngest of six brothers, and his mother doted on him until she died. He expected the same of his wife. Papa could barely abide Mama's daily ritual. The sun rose on her kneeling morning prayers and set with her kneeling devotions. Mama's devotion to God flew in the face of Papa's belief that he was eternally damned. Mama drove his feelings deeper whenever she reminded him, "Your Christmas and Easter attendance will not save your soul from the eternal fires of hell, Mr. Kabel."

"No more children." Dr. Shoal told Papa after my birth. Mama was in bed four months with Dr. Shoal's weekly visits. The neighbors helped with cooking and washing. Mama was well liked and everyone was concerned as lingering days left her weaker and weaker and her eyes sunk back into her face deeper and deeper despite the daily ox-tail soup Dr. Shoal ordered. Mrs. Headapohl birthed a child after I was born and became pregnant again before Mama could sit at the dining room table. Mama's illness scared Papa into abstinence.

~ ~ ~ ~ ~ ~

An odious hatred of Harold filled me and pumped through my body one beat at a time. I knew when Mama saw my head she would also hate Harold.

"Take off your clothes and go stand under that pipe." Harold snatched me off the chair, pointed to a far corner then retreated behind the curtain. The cot squeaked under his weight, and the sound of a popped cork followed. The smell of his noxious farts hurried me to the other corner. Naked, I prayed Harold's soul dwell eternally in perdition as I stood under a halo of a pipe punctured with tiny holes.

A lad, close to James Junior's age, entered the room carrying a stack of clothes. He whistled happily and smiled as he laid his burden on a wooden chair. I watched as he snatched up my discarded clothing. He took two steps and opened a small, blackened door in the wall and hurled my clothes into dancing orange flames. In a flash, my possessions were furnace ashes. Tasks done, he rolled up his sleeves, reached over my head and jerked on a dangling chain. His action baptized me with thin pin pricks of water needles. In a weak attempt to protect itself, my forty-pound frame shivered to bring heat to the forefront. The punishing cold water separated into thin rivulets and disappeared into a small open drain at my feet. My teeth rattled. I clasped my hands tightly in front of myself and wished Mama would come through the door.

Chain released, water stopped the lad wielded a long-handled pig-bristle brush and circled me in a ring-around-the-rosy fashion turning my flesh into angry, red welts. A circumference complete, the lad pulled the chain and released another thin sheet of ice water needles, which failed to completely rinse the caustic brown lye soap from me. "No lice," he announced, "Dress." I hated him too.

My new clothes lay on the other side of the cold, wet floor. No towel awaited me. Mama always warmed my towel on the kitchen mantel, while I bathed Saturdays in a washtub of kettle-heated water as I played with canal boats that Papa had whittled. They were brightly painted colors and bore familiar names of the Miami-Erie Canal traffic. My favorite was the purple Marymae. Her Captain Spencer allowed my brothers to tie her up at Third Street pier. "Practice boys," he would say, "I'll be back and hire you on."

My underwear did the work of a towel, and I rubbed myself making the wet briefs almost impossible to slide up my legs. The cloth clung to my knobby knees like the shell of a departed cicada clung to a summer tree. "Hurry," I told myself. I didn't want to keep Papa waiting. I added the shirt and faced a real problem. I was a neophyte when it came to buttons. My homespuns were buttonless because Mama deposited buttons in her round painted lilac jar the way others deposit money in the bank.

On Saturday sundown Mama always served a cold supper of cornbread and milk. Papa, James Junior and Puddin would crudely crumble their bread and toss it in the milk and gulp it down. Mama and I were more genteel. We buttered our bread and washed it down our throats proportionately, alternating bites of bread with sips of milk. When the grandfather clock chimed eight, Papa stood, walked to the back door and there braced his hand against the back door until the seventh chime sounded, and wordless he left. My brothers hastily left out the front door. Mama winked at me and went to her sideboard. I can see her now posed in front of the mahogany buffet, her most prized piece of furniture in our house. The drawers were empty of linens but contained her grandmother's dishes and silverware. I can see the petticoat mirror at the console's bottom, reflecting Mama's skirt. There she waited and did not move until the unoiled back gate hinge synchronized her action. She was free to perform 'Button Dump'. Her Saturday night ritual.

Ceremoniously, Mama dumped her buttons over the dining room table, sat, closed her eyes and gently worked her treasure as far and wide as their number allowed. Her face was celestial. Finished, she flung open her eyes and giggled mischievously as if she had rearranged the stars. "Take count."

Carefully, I tallied with the same preciseness I counted her egg money. Touching each button with adulation of rosary beads, I fulfilled my duty. Mama waited lovingly watching over me. Her face was celestial and when I finished, she flung open her arms. "Tell me."

I told her the amount and she would select a button, hold it up and begin her story of the button's history. Mama was a great storyteller and it didn't matter if her audience numbered one. "This one, I sliced with my trowel. It was hidden in my garden soil and I sliced right through the little thing." Then she would remind me that things often were not perfect, but everything was important. "Look, Theo. It no longer is able to hook things together but its opalescence gives a beautiful rainbow to the pearlized shell." I could see the rainbow.

"This button was lying on my father's headstone at Calvary Cemetery. Mama's eyes glistened as she held the black onyx button up to the gaslight. Sadness weighted her words. "I knelt to retrieve this button and your Papa thought I swooned. He yanked me to my feet so fast we both toppled over the steep hillside. Father Osterday never stopped the benediction as people rushed to help us." She paused and looked at something my eyes could never see. I gently touched her arm. It startled her and she jumped back in her story. "Theo, I know it was a message from my Papa. A message from the other side." Her smile was angelic.

"Your Papa tried to tell me it was lost mourning jewelry of a widow attending her family graves. He called me silly." Then Mama turned full face to me and winked, drawing me into her cabal. I believed with her the message was from my grandfather.

Lifting the largest button, a yellow ocher, black-tinged tortoise shell, Mama pressed it to her cheek, then laid it on my opened palm and lovingly stroked it allowing her slender fingers to slide off mine. "Furiously, I worked this pretty from between the rails at Third and Main Streets. My heart pounded in my chest as an oncoming horse-cart bore down on me. The clop, clop of horses' hooves and the metal carriage wheels grew louder as I remained on the track, bent over and wiggling the button. People shouted for me to jump aside. The conductor clanged his bell as if it were Judgment Day but I kept working on the button." Mama flung her head backwards and her sand red curls flew free from her chignon pins. The curls bobbed around her face like freed clock springs and she gulped air. Perspiration dewed her upper lip with the telling of the story and the silence between us lengthened. I nervously swung my legs back and forth. Mama savored the moment then released softly, "A very handsome man with cinnamon eyes and dove-colored hair that curled from under his dashing black bowler pulled me up on my feet. He pressed his camel hair coat and wrapped me tightly in his arms lifting me off the ground. He removed me from the tracks. Theo, the horse's tail brushed my cheek as he galloped past us." A warmth came in her eyes at the memory.

"Oh Mama." The hairs on my neck rose to think of it.

She radiated as she continued. "We stood beside the rails and I stared into his laughing eyes. His dimples deepened and we were surrounded by applause from both sides of the track." Mama crossed her arms over her chest, grasped the ends of her shoulders and hugged her memory. Something in her shifted. She spoke now to herself. "He raised my clenched fist with his large kid-gloved hand and gently pried open my fingers." Taking back the button from me, she said, "I opened my fist and this button stuck to the end of my finger tip. He laughed until his entire body shook. We stood, he and I, like two fools laughing in the middle of Main Street. Someone yelled, 'Kiss him. He saved your life.' I pecked him on the cheek and thanked him. We turned away and walked off in different directions." Mama's face fell sad and she slowed her breathing.

"Oh, Mama, you were so brave."

Her spine stiffened. The warmth of the kitchen cooled. She gently brushed back the curls from her face and stared at me. "Do not say that. It was foolhardy. Had I been killed I would never have you."

The back gate squeaked Papa's return. She scraped the table clean of buttons and placed them hurriedly in her jar and then placed a round pearl button in the center as if she was putting a cherry on a cupcake. She returned the jar to the sideboard.

~ ~ ~ ~ ~ ~

I cast my memory aside and finished dressing in my uniform. I pulled suspenders up on my narrow shoulders where they quickly slid off and rested at my elbows. I put my feet in the high-laced shoes and lastly stuffed my arms in the gray collarless jacket. I topped myself with a matching gray cap and stepped to the mirror.

Mama said it was a sin to feel vainglorious. I am deep in sin. I loved how I looked. I loved having new shoes. Maybe the price of the hair cut was worth the cost. I went over to the black leather barber chair, and I grabbed two fists full of my curls and stuffed my pockets.

CHAPTER 4: BEHIND THE WALLS

I was placed at the head of a long line and dropped to my knees with an immediate kidney punch. "Captain, Sir. He won't know what to do." Captain nodded and the bully stepped over me and claimed back his right to line leader. A bell rang, transforming our line into a centipede of marching feet. I staggered to my feet and stumbled along behind the bully. When he stopped behind his chair, I halted at the chair beside him. The entire time my eyes searched the mess hall for my brothers.

On cue, everyone took a seat. The loud scrapping of chair legs hurt my ears. Seated, we raised a spoon to a jousting position, waiting for what, I don't know. Ah, another bell permitted the lowering of spoons into our bowls of very thin bonny clabber. We ate in silence. I swizzled my spoon troweling for spaetzles. Swirling the broth, I futilely searched for the little buttery, dumplings Mama laced in our clabber. Not finding any I turned to my tablemate and asked, "Do we get sec…" Before I finished my question the bully hit the back of my head with a stunning blow and I fell from my chair, dazed. A fourth bell brought the diners to their feet, and I fought my way up to stand on wobbly legs. I felt the lump on my head, grabbed my bowl and spoon and slurped my way down the aisle between the long running tables to the waiting hogshead. With a toss of my dinnerware, I added tin notes to the symphony of the receiving barrels.

A white aproned inmate in a matching hair net grabbed my arm. "Baby, is you still hungry?" I stopped. "Do not eat after the fourth bell, do not slurp from your bowl, do not eat after we stand, do not eat while walking, Knot Head." He punched my stomach and folded me in half. I remember being on the floor and he was standing on my chest. Where is James Junior? When I opened my mouth to scream, I received a choking mouthful of scraped slop from the scrapings of his spoon. I gagged. "No, no. No noise and no lip from you shithead. And if you puke on my floor, I'll pull your eyes out through your ass." He moved his foot up to my throat. I heard distant laughing just as the room went black. The apron lifted his foot and kicked my ribs. The next thing I saw was Captain's shoes in front of me. I struggled to my knees and he lifted me to my feet. I moaned. "Newbie, slipped in his own slop," Apron told Captain, shrugged and turned his back.

Captain shoved me into the back hall where I became the last legs of the marching centipede. We passed a door painted in large red capital letters. I stopped to sound out the word, "SOLITARY." Captain shoved me again and I twisted to give him the stink eye. He slapped my back and yelled, "Eyes forward!" His shove launched me into the backyard where shadows lengthened across ruts made by orphans' feet in the rigors of 'Run-Goosey-Run, Kick-The-Can and many innings of baseball. The grass was beaten back into Mother Earth leaving boundary lines straighter than ruled chalk lines. The backyard belied the manicured front lawn. It walled in abandon children who were meant to be society's invisible. Life behind the walls of the backyard was Dayton's dirty secret.

"I'm Thomas." Captain held out his hand. He cast a shadow the length of James Junior but was not as broad. I would not look at him. He laid his hand on my shoulder and followed my gaze. "That is where the Negro children live." I snapped my head in the other direction. "That is the Infirmary. Don't go there. Kids go in and never come out. Guinea pigs. They are used for medical experiments." His voice cracked and I whirled on his weakness.

"Listen, I don't know what Infirmary means, but I

see it sits next to the girls' dorm and I've been warned to stay out of there." I gave a hard look and he laughed at me. He rubbed my cap which drove me straight into fighting anger. "You gobshite." Thomas placed his palm on my forehead, and I windmilled the air between us. I screamed and cried until my arms dropped listlessly at my sides.

"Temper, little man." Tears burned my eyes and I took back up arm flailing. Captain stood his ground at arm's length, his hand on my forehead. I could have churned two pounds of butter in the length of time I swung at Captain. I stopped thrashing and he dropped to the ground. I lept on his back. He stood and spun me until I fell off his back. Thump, I hit the ground. I had lost my senses of sight, sound and feel. Smelling my nosebleed and tasting my blood remained with me.

"Look, kid, I am just trying to be a friend."

"I don't need you. I have brothers. You didn't help when the line leader punched me or when that apron bastard made me swallow slop he scooped out of the barrel. I don't need you."

"But you will, little man. You will."

"Stop calling me Little Man. My brothers will beat you and every other bastard that hurts me." I knew I promised something I could not deliver. I gave Thomas a wispy blow to his stomach.

His hands went up like a prizefighter addressing the referee. "Ok, big Man. I do not see your brothers rescuing you. Where are they?" Sulking, I lowered my head. His words stung and I pushed out my bottom bleeding lip and thought about what he said. I didn't have brother backup. "Do you have a name?"

"Theophilus Kabel." Thomas did not laugh at my name. "My family call me Theo," I gave him the invitation. He extended his hand again and we shook.

"Ok, Theo. There are things you should know. First, the orphanage has a network of rats or snitches. Authorities will believe a snitch and never you. Pick your friends wisely." He paused letting his words sink in. "The building over there is laundry and ironing building. Big boys sweat off their balls in there. The heat drains the bully out of them. Your brothers might be working in there. We grow our own food over there in the garden. You will work there tomorrow, and you need to know if a plant is trampled every boy in the dorm will be thrashed. Code of Honor demands no one rats on a dormmate. If you tell you will be thrown downstairs. You must remain true to the Code in order to survive. The staff thrashes the entire dorm if no one gives up a name, but thrashings are best done when done to all. The beater's arm tires, don't you see?"

"I never thought about thrashings. I've never been thrashed. Papa just knuckles my brothers a blow to the head."

Thomas sadly smiled. "You'll learn Code demands older boys take the first beating. Little ones like you go last." Thomas locked his eyes on mine. "Beatings hurt, but if your cry and scream like they are killing you, they go easier. Don't be a hard head for authority. But be a hard ass for bullies. Will you have visitors?"

I laughed. "I ain't staying. My Papa will be back in the morning. I am just here for a haircut and some new clothes. Look I have new shoes, not ever used." I was truly proud of my shoes.

Thomas saddened, "Oh, Theo. You don't know?"

My life fell into a rabbit warren that I did not understand. Thomas hung his head because he could not look me in the eyes. "I am sorry, Theo. This is your home now." I felt as hollow as a milkweed pod. Afraid, I moved closer to Thomas. Night closed on day and the hens clucked in their nests. My stomach heaved and I hurled curdled milk over the tops of my shoes while Thomas rubbed my back. "Homesick," he said. "The cruelest disease of all. The Asylum breeds it and everybody comes down with it. You never recover. Today is your worse day, I promise. Homesickness will burrow inside you until you think it is dormant. Then a memory or a smell triggers an onset. Unpredictable, homesickness fancies its own sweet will."

"Mama has chickens."

"See what I mean? The clucking chickens tossed you a memory of home and squeezed the contents of your stomach tighter than a vise." Thomas was right. He smiled and pulled me to him, and we made our own silence in the middle of raised voices calling, "Your Out, Ollie-ollie-in-free, You're Safe."

"Now, Theo, listen very carefully. This is the most important thing to know. If you hit a ball out of the yard, never chase it. Let it go. A kid tried to climb the fence along Munger Avenue and he was shot. The fence is a line of death and the staff have rifles." Color drained south of his face and his eyes were cold and hard. His forehead furrowed into deep lines and his mouth set ugly. He squeezed me hard. "But hey, when you are twelve you can become a Trustee." He was grinning from ear to ear. "Pimply Old Harold was known to visit The Silver Fox, a bar on Third Street. He filled his jug years ago before his leg gave out on him, so he pays Trustees to tote his empty jugs to the Fox for a refill. Now when I say pay, it isn't money. No, Harold allows sips of suds to the walker of his jugs. Don't let Dayhoff catch you sipping. So see, you have something in which to look forward, Old Man. That is, if you keep your nose clean."

"Thomas, I ain't going to be here long enough to become a Trustee." The bell rang me back into the centipede where my steps fell into the cadence, and I beamed at my ability to march. Thomas showed me my bed in our dorm. I was at the end of a long line of white-sheeted cots. Each cot bridged a wooden box. Thomas pulled my box out and told me to swap out of my clothes for the nightshirt. Afterwards the boys knelt and I followed moving my lips in silence to the unknown prayer. Dormmates quickly jumped into bed leaving me to pull and yank at my covers. My actions amused the room while tears dammed my sight. Thomas came to me and lifted the top sheet. "Slide in."

"Two sheets?" My question set up a howl in the room. I had no idea. At home, we slept on a bare tick mattress. James' long legs were my cover. He and Puddin slept lengthwise, side-by-side on the iron bed, and I slept crossways at the bottom of their smelly feet.

Tonight the moon shared its light across my bed. I was thankful. The door opened and I sat up to the hall shadow of a man standing in our doorway. "Papa?" I called.

"Lay down, Newbie," bawled the shadow and then walked toward me the length of our cots. Frightened I flattened myself. Was this a walking thrashing for me? Whack! My feet hanging off my bed were stung by a night stick. I yelped.

"Captain?"

"Eighteen, Sir."

"Eighteen." The night walking man confirmed and retreated becoming a hall shadow still watching us. Silently he closed the door and the boys got out of bed and ran around whispering and snatching each other's comic book contraband.

"He will be back," Captain Thomas warned just as the door flew open and the shadow grew in the doorway. Whack! His stick struck the doorframe causing the windows to rattle. Boys belly busted into beds that did not belong to them. I lay stiff as a freshly graved corpse.

"Captain, control your ladies or I will."

"Yes, Sir." The light in the hall went out taking the shadow. No one moved for ten minutes. A metal click in the dark affirmed the door's closing. Whispers jumped around the room. "Shut up, you little turds. If he returns I won't save your ass." Thomas threw out the threat.

"If he comes back. You won't have to. It will be your ass, Captain, Sir. " Threat returned.

CHAPTER 5: TRAIN RIDE

Papa did not visit once in the two years of our homogenous days of thrashings and thin broth. He merely showed up and collected us with as much emotion as a farmer collected hen house eggs. Summoned to the parlor, we watched a faded memory conduct himself as though he checked us in the previous day. I realized I had forgotten the details of his face. We three boys lined up single file and followed the recollection I had stashed in the dark corner of my mind. We passed the starch-faced matron who inked us into hell on our arrival and was now hatefully abolishing our names and our tuition. She donned the scowl of Satan.

As we neared the Great Miami River, I was overcome by the smell. I was overcome by the smell because it either evoked homesickness for bygone days or it saturated me with a divine feeling of freedom. I was going home. Just as deeply sadness came to me. I was forced to depart the asylum without saying goodbye to Thomas. Did they tell him I was reclaimed? Did he know they forbid children from saying goodbye to friends? I felt I was deserting him. First thing, I am going to speak to Mama about bringing Thomas to live with us. He is a good worker and he is honest, I will tell her. I will share my food with him. He won't be an expense. Heck, I've gotten used to not eating much. Mama, I can hardly wait to see her. To see her new buttons.

Spiders spin webs to hide their eggs. Papa spun webs to hide our eight Asylum seasons. In a fabric of thick, stringy webbing of prattle, he made no mention of James Junior's height. James had grown taller than Papa. He did not mention Puddin's added weight. Unnoticeable were the changes in me 'cause I was different inside. My world was turned upside down. Papa put me in the midst of a pack of wild children. I was separated from my brothers, and I was frightened in the kennel of kids. The untamed group lied, bit and beat me. I hated this man walking us home. I hated him for the daily beatings. If it showed in my eyes, he never once looked into the hatred.

At Fifth and Wilkinson, Papa stopped in front of Burkitt's Apothecary. Colonel William Burkitt and Papa were Lincoln's men in the Great War. Doc Burkitt brought cherry liniment when Papa was laid up with gout. Mama placed a cherry smelling compress across Papa's swollen toes, and Papa cursed life, neighbors, and the weather. But he never cursed in the presence of Aunt Love.

Our neighbor Aunt Love was an old maid schoolteacher. Papa cut wood for her and we boys stacked it for her on her back porch. She rewarded us in pies, cakes and fudge. Sugar was an 'unnecessary' on our grocery bill. One night Aunt Love fell in her yard when she returned from her out-house. The fall broke her hip. She laid in her yard all night, not wanting to holler and wake us. Mama brought her to our house to heal.

"Her pelvic girdle has healed crooked." Doc Clark told my parents she would never walk again.

Doc Burkitt ordered her a moveable chair, the kind being used by the Great War veterans. It was a high reaching, cane-back chair with large wooden spokes on the side wheels that dwarfed her diminutive size. Aunt Love lived in her chair. She ate in it and slept there. I was in awe of Aunt Love. She was magic. She grew a third set of teeth which I thought was magical, and her best magic was when she wheeled herself. Like the silent flight of an owl, she came in the room and cast a spell on Papa. She put a ceasefire on Papa streaking the air blue with cussing.

Doc Burkitt and Aunt Love were coconspirators.

They drew up a blueprint of deceit directly under Mama's nose. I loved watching their game. Doc Burkitt entered with a grand gesture of "Good evening, Aunt Love." He sang it in his Saturday night, bel canto voice. Aunt Love batted her eyes coyly and demurely lowered her head. Doc would lean over her chair, blocking Mama's view with his rotund basso body. "How are you?" He continued on a perfect note of A flat.

"Fair to middle, thank you." Quickly, she turned her thin, blue-veined wrist upward to receive a packet dropped in her black mourning handkerchief, and then she folded the embroidered white 'L' corner over the packet. Doc Burkitt patted her shoulder just long enough for Aunt Love to slip the hanky up her long sleeve. Fait accompli, Doc lumbered away. Mama hated snuff.

Doc Burkitt grieved the loss of his mother. She died shortly before the ending of the Great War and it broke his heart. He blamed himself for not being there to care for her at the time. "Every son should be allowed to lay his mother to rest." Those were the strongest words he used against Mr. Lincoln who denied all furlough requisitions during the most critical time in the war, its ending. Doc grieved deeply for what he could not change. His steely eyes softened after the war, and his strong face melted into the sad jowls of a Bassett hound. His looks added deeply to his emotional Saturday night performances at Turner Opera House.

~ ~ ~ ~ ~ ~

We entered Burkitt's Apothecary, Perfumery and Fancy Articles where a trio of regulars sat against the back wall warming their feet on a cast iron stove. "Doc's on an errand." One of the men called. Papa nodded.

James Junior, Puddin and I stopped mid-aisle of two store-length counters gorged with salves, mustard plasters, poultices and balms. On the glass countertops were binges of loose-leaf tobacco for cigarette rolling and chaw making. Hung like a pendant in the middle of the aisle was one light bulb illuminating brilliant colored apothecary jars of gold yellow, Nile green, blazing apple and piercing aquamarine. Maybe I could ask for just one jar for Mama's dressing table. Maybe Doc could order her a set. Papa nudged me on down the aisle.

A white, frocked clerk with black greasy hair stepped up to the candy case. "Show me your money."

His insult drew James Junior's attention. He moved up behind me, where I knelt. Taut tension of racehorse speed stretched out between their eyes. James Junior took it into his head that their orphanage apparel was the match that lit the remark. "We are your only customers." He challenged.

Undaunted, the clerk countered, "I have lots of work in the back. My time cannot be wasted." He turned his back on James Junior and mumbled just beyond our hearing.

"Hey! My little brother needs time. He is slow." James Junior circled his forefinger around his ear. He gave the impression I was daft and stepped aside. I tackled him and the scuffle was on.

"Stop!" Papa yelled. All of us stopped. James Junior, me and the clerk. "I am talking to you." Papa jabbed his finger at the clerk. "Colonel Burkitt's absence appears to have brought out the unhelpfulness in you, and I am sure he will not be happy to hear about your rudeness to his favorite customers, Sam." Papa's hard voice changed Sam's thinking. He needed the job. His demeanor changed and he straightened his spine, grabbed a brown sack and stepped up to the counter wearing a newly painted on smile. He had not seen Papa. "I am truly sorry for my abruptness, Mr. Kabel."

"Pick three pieces, sons." Papa smiled falsely at Sam.

"H-H-Horehound." Stuttering lassoed my tongue. When I saw the candy lifted from behind the glass it was smaller.

"No, M-M-Make that Maple Nut." The three pieces did not fill half of the clerk's hand. "N-N-No. R-R-Red licorice whips." My choice was as red as Sam's ears and half the size.

My brothers ordered. Sam folded the three bags, measured string, cut and tied off each bag of candy. He scooped up the bags and turned to hand them over. "Double the order." Papa delivered his coup de grâce. Sam's eyes slitted as he opened his mouth. Papa cleared his throat, pulled out his fob and checked the time while Sam oscillated. Three times he opened his mouth, then turned away and hinged his mouth on his words, turned back and opened his mouth and turned away hinging his word. The fanning action did not cool the red burning in his elephant ears.

Papa looked up from his timepiece, turned his back on Sam and looked to the door. "Hurry, Sam. We have a train to catch." Sam's chiseled glare was harder than the nearby marble fudge table.

Calmly, Sam set down the bags, grabbed the scissors and cut the string from the bolt. Each of the three cuts he made nipped pieces of flesh from his index finger. Red blood dripped down his white frock. He forced the candy into the last bag with such force it broke and my licorice landed on the floor. Sam looked ready to turn on the waterworks. Papa heard the bag rip and turned on Sam with eyes daring him to retrieve the spilled candy. Sam threw up a dam between his brain and his mouth. Vicious thoughts could not be spoken. His mistake would be docked from his pay. He grabbed a large bag and gently dropped in red whips taken from the case.

Crow's curse on Sam. I seethed in unspoken anger that matched Sam's. I was two times away from my favorite choice and I was two times the amount.

Moreover, my nerves brought out the stuttering in me. I might as well soil myself as to stutter publicly. My stuttering began in the Asylum. Thomas said I would outgrow it. I didn't believe him and I just showed I was right. "Pog mah thoin." I cussed.

My brothers laughed. The Irishmen leaning against the back red brick wall dropped the front legs of their chairs to the floor and laughed. Papa overlooked swearing in his native tongue feeling most did not know what it meant. He forbid us to swear in English because he said, "It makes you sound like a low class immigrant." Kiss my ass was overlooked and we left.

On the corner of South Wilkinson and Sixth Streets stood Majestic Italian Renaissance Colonnades thrust up to heaven and arched back down to earth. Around us, people scurried about their business. "Look at the unwashed masses. Oblivious." Papa synchronized his watch to the clock tower. Slow wagons pulled dockside and men unloaded crates. Horses relieved of burdens snorted relief. "Grand, isn't she?" Papa left no room for answers. "All this beauty wasted on these miserable people wallowing in their habitual ruts. None look up nor take notice of the grandeur. They could be standing at God's altar and not one person would notice." His gold fob went back in his vest pocket and he raised his voice and pointed. "Round top stood over there. She was razed for the colonnades. Round top was an ugly train station, but she had great personality. First of all she was built out of Dayton's on-site clay. Long and sturdy, she was laced up in a roof of barrel-stays. Round Top straddled three tracks with the kind of power you find in a mistress."

My brothers jerked their heads away from Papa's remark. They stared up at the clock tower. Lost in the self-imposed importance of his own words, Papa never noticed the boys' change in color. "Round Top had six, beef end doors. She scotched engineers' wheels by slamming her doors on Saturday night. She countermanded any train who ever thought of passing through her. Saturday six o'clock she bolted her doors, and they stayed locked until Monday morn evaporated Sunday's dew."

Papa rechecked the time, walked a circle around us following his thoughts. "Since Round Top was replaced one hundred and twenty-five trains slide through Dayton whenever they damn well choose to do so. Clickety, Clack. They throw cinders at church windows and belch soot on people's Sunday Best. Trains thunder through sermons throwing off cinders and drowning voices of choirs. Train whistle's scream agitates patients at St. Elizabeth Hospital. Is that progress? They say progress lies in a Time Table. Damnfools." He spat.

I was bug-eyed at his talk. Papa was a man who never kept a Holy Day of Obligation, never prayed a rosary and a Novena was foreign to him. Papa was a man who long since held his sins from a confession. Now he was railing against train travel on Sunday, and his words were lost on me and my brothers. They rolled their eyes. Maybe he grew quiet because he sensed he'd lost influence over our thinking. His eyes became very dark and he dropped the subject as if he had startled himself as well as us.

~ ~ ~ ~ ~ ~

The sound of an oncoming train moved us to the nearly empty platform. The black locomotive bearing down on us frightened me and I grabbed Puddin's hand. Eerily the wheels screamed as the brakes locked them down and curling snakes of smoke lurched from beneath the train and coiled around my ankles. I jumped back and yanked Puddin off balance. A black-suited conductor with brass buttons and a small cap stepped off the train, right where we stood. A porter followed and set a metal footstool on the ground. Pressing both hands against my overflowing pockets, I climbed the stool steps. Behind me, my brothers jumped. Never touching the stool they lit on the train steps taking them two at a time, just to show me up. James Junior pushed me aside while Papa talked to the conductor outside our window. James Junior claimed a window seat. Puddin plopped beside him. I stood in the aisle until Papa came in and pushed two moveable seat backs forward so that he and I could ride backwards facing the brothers. Papa's knees touched James Junior's long legs and yet he did not mention his son's growth. He did not even mention Mama.

Two short whistles announced our departure. I turned to the window and watched passing buildings as we picked up speed. We crossed roads and aggravated horse riders. We delighted children along the way, and they waved as if we should know them. One cocky horseman kicked his ride until fear rolled the horse's eyes white as the two beat us across an intersection. I chewed my licorice.

"Ditch lilies." Papa winced and reached across me, raised our window and hollered at the orange-flamed flowers clumped in nests along the track. "Ditch lilies." He screwed up his face. His neck veins rose and spread red. We were used to him addressing Mama's backyard garden in such a manner. Sleeping people opened their eyes on his tirade. "I ate those nasty tubers roasted, boiled in creek water soup. I ate them sliced and fried in fat-back. I ate them raw because we had to march through many a mealtime," he said sourly ignoring the stares. Papa hated the flowers more vehemently than he hated Copperheads. His continued his war on Mama's garden.

"You should be grateful God made Tiger Lilies. They provided you nourishment that kept you from starving." All the while she planted more and more long-throated tiger lilies in her garden. And Papa continued to advance upon them, spit on them and curse them. He shut the backyard gate on their stray blossoms and leaves, perpetuating my parent's not-so-unspoken war.

Papa's words drove in my ears. My sugar-coated brain drowned them out. I just wanted to see Mama. The swaying of our car carried me off to sleep, and I dreamed of Mama holding me once again.

"Xenia." The words cracked open my dream, and I opened my eyes in a new surrounding. Confused, I looked around then realized we were at our destination. Maybe Mama would be waiting on the platform. We stepped off the train at a very strange station that sat in the biggest mess of pig-iron. Tracks were thrown down like Pick-Up-Stix in all directions. It was completely opposite of Dayton's organized alignment of an east-west fashion.

"Xenia Station is laid out like a mourning dove's nest. God's worst nest-making bird," Papa said as we jumped over tracks. We hailed a farmer who had come into town to deliver his hay. His wagon was pulled by a horse wearing a hat with ear holes that I thought made him look surprisingly regal.

"Where to?" asked the driver as Papa climbed up on his bench. James lifted me up on the wagon bed, and I sat between him and Puddin. We dangled our legs and stuck straw in our mouths and pretended to puff on it.

"Poverty Hill." Papa said.

CHAPTER 6: OHIO SOLDIERS AND SAILORS ORPHANAGE

"Our twenty homelike cottages have great light and ventilation. We have a hospital, school and chapel. The Grand Army of the Republic, in which you served, Mr. Kabel, supports us. I will be glad to acquaint you with our facility, Sir."

Papa stood at parade rest. "That won't be necessary, Colonel. Sir."

"Sir, do you have any questions?" Superintendent Colonel Simon's military eyes inspected Papa who foundered in awkward silence. Mute, Papa shook his downward cast head. The silence grew longer. Colonel Simon waited. "Well then, if you have none, take a seat and we will complete the paperwork." Papa sat. "Sir, the children's names?"

"James Kabel Junior. Puddin . . .excuse me, George Kabel and Theophilus Kabel."

My mouth dropped open. Oh no!

"Their last residence, Sir?"

"528 Summit Street, Dayton, Ohio."

Colonel Simon's head came up. He stopped writing and stared at Papa. "The Children's Asylum?" Papa nodded. I yelled and James shoved me behind him. "Sir, are you the father?" He received another silent nod from the man who talked the entire trip over here. The Colonel squared his shoulders, drummed his fingers on his desk as he surveyed us. Thinking he had not been understood, he said, "Sir, I mean is that their current address. Today's address?"

"Y-y-yes, Sir."

Colonel Simon shook his head. "Your full name?" His voice had a tight timbre and he dropped his respected 'Sir'.

"J-J-James K-K-Kabel, S-S-Senior." I laughed out

loud. There was my stutter. Now he is nervous. James Junior covered my mouth as Papa turned to stare.

"He laughs when he gets nervous." James Junior said. I pushed away his hand and stopped laughing.

Colonel Simon nodded in understanding. Papa's face boiled in fury. He clenched his fists.

"Your military Service and Disability?"

Well kiss me bollocks. Someone realizes he is disabled. If you ask me bollocks, he is disabled in the brain and you can take that to the blarney stone.

"101st. Ohio Volunteer Infantry, Company F. And 8th Ohio Cavalry, Company E." Papa blurted proudly.

"That was your service?" Colonel Simon said curtly. "And your disability?"

"R-R-Rheu-m-m-m-matism." That took forever to answer.

"And?" Colonel Simon added, "Is that all on your papers?"

Unable to answer, Papa shook his head. Colonel Simon waited. My brothers held their breath. I snickered behind my hand. The Old Man was getting his dressing down and I was enjoying his displayed weakness.

"P-P-Piles. S-S-Sir." I thought too late now Old Man to act like you have respect for anyone.

"Pension?"

Colonel Simon continued taking the Old Man lower than his bollocks. Now he was forced to divulge his wallet. He looked down at his hands, twisted his back to us, slid his Adam's apple up under his graybeard, leaned into Simon's desk and whispered. "Six dollars monthly."

"Mother's date of death?"

"December 2, 1891."

My knees collapsed and the floor rose. "Mama!" I screamed. The room went down a tiny black hole. Unconscious, I urinated on myself.

"Stand like a man." I heard from far away. I moved

up on my knees. Colonel Simon stepped from behind his desk and demanded my father unhand me. I fell back to the floor where I sobbed snot and tears into my puddle of urine. "Mama."

Graybeard snatched me up, yelling, "No son of mine will swoon like a sissy."

Colonel Simon shoved Graybeard against the wall.

"You bastard." I shrank into a ball dangling off my father's arm as he reached around Colonel Simon and flung me against the desk. I slid off to the floor like spittle juice slid off his chaw. My brothers circled me. James Junior picked me up and pressed my head to his shoulder. "Leave him alone, you gobshite." My father froze, his fist in mid air. Puddin cooed soft words to my back but my brain was senseless.

Angrily, Colonel Simon spun around and pushed the papers across his desk. "Sign here." Low was his opinion of the man who put him in the position of revealing a mother's death to her unsuspecting child, and he wanted the man gone from his office and out of the child's life.

"Stand up to him," I cried tear-choked words. James Junior could Indian Wrestle Old Graybeard and pin the bastard to the ground. James held me tighter and pretended not to hear. Finished with his signing us out of his life, Old Graybeard extended Puddin his hand. Puddin shook it. James Junior kept his arms wrapped around me. His accusing eyes fixed on Old Graybeard who dared not offer his hand.

Graybeard turned on his heel and walked out of our lives for the second time. Junior put me down. "God kill him," I said and vomited red earthworm-looking licorice. I was seven months, three weeks and a day shy of my sixth birthday.

~ ~ ~ ~ ~ ~

Ohio Soldier and Sailor Orphanage aligned itself

with state procedure. Shave heads, shower nits, new clothes. This time I abandoned clothes with no-never-mind knowing Mama's fingers never touched the Asylum clothes. She never brushed crumbs from the shirtfront or squeezed laundry water out of the britches. She never draped them on the grape arbor and they never smelled like sunshine. I felt nothing at their leave taking. And I never spoke "Papa" again. "Piss on the clothes! Piss on Old Graybeard."

~ ~ ~ ~ ~ ~

"You are Home Cadets." A headless man shouted through a megaphone. "I am Colonel Simon." The megaphone dropped away and he was no longer headless. I turned my chin to my shoulder and admired my new uniform with chevrons and braids. "This is Phibbs."

A fierce-looking man stood. His severe mouth was mustached in a straight line of black hair, and his spine made a lightning rod look curved. The glare of Phibbs' spit-shined shoes made eyes squint. Sergeant Phibbs caught each orphan's face in the artillery of his eyes as he counted a full sixty seconds. No cadet moved under Phibbs' scrutiny. "Our mission is to help each of you make something of yourself. Don't cuss. Don't use tobacco. And remember decorum will be required at all times. Your behavior will be exemplary. At the sound of the bugle you will ready for class. Presence in a classroom outside school hours is forbidden. Prompt and willing obedience must be given to all orders." Phibbs' words hit us like artillery fire as he paced the length of the stage, giving a rover eye to each and every cadet. I don't think anyone dared breathe until he said, "There will be no corporal punishment."

What the hell? Are you kidding? Would you repeat that? I thought.

"Unless it is an extreme case of disobedience and would cause harm to yourself or others."

Harm? I wondered. Is a kidney punch harm? Does stepping on another's throat constitute harm?

"Graduation requires you learn a trade. If you are unable to learn a trade you will be sent to Columbus Asylum of the Feeble Minded."

Oh gobshite! Wonder if I can learn a trade.

Pausing, Sergeant Phibbs fingered his moustache the way a lion paws his whiskers before devouring his prey. He executed an 'about-face' and headed back my way describing the trades. "We have a print shop, a bindery, a tin shop and a cobbler house. We sole shoes. We make shoes for cadets and staff. We have a tailor shop and we teach carpentry. We have a blacksmith." He bragged about the livery providing heavy shoes for the horses and tiny anvils the livery made to extract baby teeth. He praised the Agriculture course. "Future farmers are in the field producing crops bountiful enough to feed the Home and run a Saturday market in tow." Sergeant Phibbs closed with a description of butchers and bakers.

"How 'bout candlestick maker?" I shouted. Ensuing laughter bathed over me and I grinned back. Sergeant Phibbs' was stone-faced for the length of time it took the cadets to come to their senses. My guardian angel stopped me short of taking a bow just as one-armed Sergeant Phibbs landed in front of me. He flew off the stage and landed with barely a sound.

"No, you will not be a candlestick maker, Mr. Rub-A-Dub-Dub, Three Kabels-in-a-tub."

Kiss me bollocks, he knew us. James knuckled the back of my head. I fell out like a lightning-struck tree falls out of a forest. Sergeant Phibbs stepped aside for me, and I landed face down out of the forest of boys. I entered Summit Street straight as an arrow, my mother's son. I morphed into a wiseacre. I pushed my toe over the line continuously because I could. I was

Captain Thomas' buddy. No one messed with me. James entered Summit Street being a wiseacre. Graybeard's son. Summit Street rearranged both James' and my personalities as evidenced by my prone position now at Sergeant Phibbs' feet.

"Cadet Kabel, while you are down there give me ten pushups." I got right on the order. Finished, I stood. Sergeant Phibbs turned to a matron seated on the stage. "Mark Cadet Theophilus Kabel a month of no dessert."

"So noted, Sergeant."

Phibbs turned back to me. "Now to get the vinegar out of you, give me twenty-five laps around the gymnasium." As I jogged to the wall he called, "Halt. Outside, Cadet. And make it an even one-hundred. Drop your insolence outside the door."

Up to my chin in shame, a new-found emotion, I glanced to James for sympathy. I received the ugly eye.

"Let this be the last time you embarrass your family. That means all of us. We all are your family, Cadet."

I ran laps telling myself I would rather be thrashed. It was quick and finished. Beatings did not shame me. I was very uncomfortable in this new emotion. I hated the feeling of my red face. I ran laps telling myself the blush would subside but I felt it only deepening. I returned to a gymnasium of cadets who were depositing napkins. Lemonade stained their upper lips. Cookie crumbs clung to their shirt front. My lesson was hard learned.

A minister came on the stage and brought us to attention. He had a strong pulpit voice. "Religious Services will be held on Saturday afternoons in Chapel. City clergy rotate services among themselves. I think it is a great joy to preach at O.S.S.O. because we are guaranteed a full house." He laughed at his joke. Then explained to our dumbstruck faces, "Attendance is mandatory."

~ ~ ~ ~ ~ ~

A cadet in a blue uniform, modeled after West Point with the same brass buttons and no pockets, marched us across campus to Cottage 22. There the cadet introduced us to our housemother. "Mother Brush is my mother too. If you cause her trouble you will put on boxing gloves and meet me in the ring. If you win, the campus newspaper *The Home Weekly* will publish your name. If you win." His words were backed by his six-foot-three, two-hundred-pound frame and I had nothing to say.

"I am sure they will be my best brood." Our housemother looked like a sugar cookie, just as round, just as bland. She wore a coronet of fat, blond braids. Her body held no neck. Her round legs ended in ankles that draped over the sides of her black, no-nonsense shoes.

Replacing his cap, the uniform crowed. "Just let me know, Mother Brush. You know where to find me." His about-face left us in her charge. We sidled a little closer to Mother Brush. Her body radiated love and we could feel it. I quickly learned Mother Brush collected children the way a library collects books. After she studied a child's nature, she shelved the child in just the appropriate category. A Western novel would feel out of sorts on a Nursery Rhyme shelf was her belief.

Mrs. Brush's Cottage was a calm, loving safe place. We were not without rules though. NO EATING in the cottage was the first commandment I broke. Since we ate in the dining hall across campus I believe smuggled food might taste better. Mrs. Brush accompanied us to our meals, and although all the staff ate in the dining hall they took turns watching over the cadets. As in the Asylum we could not talk. But unlike the Asylum, roving staff made discipline reports. One night soon after my arrival, I hid a tablemate's unwanted corn bread under my pillow. Lights out, I began to nibble. I awoke early and brushed crumbs from my sheets. I had committed the perfect crime. That night in the dining hall Mrs. Brush detoured my pie to Christopher Williams, a lad she seemed to favor. The unspoken reason for her decision came down upon me like a thunderbolt. It struck harder than any beating I had ever received. It left my tongue chaste of the idea smuggled food was tastier. I never broke the rule twice.

Friday nights we crossed to the dining hall in double time. We came back in triple time because we were birds free of weeknight study time. Leisure hours began with a deep claw-footed tub bath. I treasured the gift almost as much as dessert. At the Asylum, I was forced to shower in-group in a massive, cold cement stall.

Ohio Soldiers and Sailors Orphanage scheduled academics for Morning School. Afternoons we had shop. James enrolled in carpentry and his class built a fence roadside along the pond where we watched bottom-feeding duck tails stick straight out of the water. Straight as cattails, the foraging ducks clustered upended. Hence the name, 'Duck-Butt-Pond' could be referred, but never did the staff allow us to make a sign for the watering hole. The class was teased for trying to fence in fish.

Puddin enrolled in the horticulture class, 'Green Thumbs' they were teased. Puddin loved working the greenhouse because he said it was like canned sun. His class was planting a long row of evergreens, roadside. The bushes were planted outside James' class fence. That was the summer the uproar began. Xenia residents took notice and called for an investigation. The *Daily Gazette* wrote a scathing report about Colonel Simon's expenditure, saying it was unnecessary. The headlines were "A Waste of Funds on Orphans". The articles kept coming and the class kept planting. The criticism united us into tightly woven comradery, or as Mama said 'woven tighter than broad cloth'. Rank and File, we entrenched our perimeter of admiration for Colonel Simon and his staff as the citizens attacked our home. We were the O.S.S.O. Army.

~ ~ ~ ~ ~ ~

Our teachers taught us to read. Mother Brush taught the love of books. She expanded my text reading to the world of magazines, comic papers and newspapers. Saturday and Sunday afternoons, I sat on her three-legged stool while she knitted and I read aloud. Proudly, I sounded out articles of local and world news. If a word stumped me, she would smile and cease knitting. She leaned her glasses into the word, pronounced the puzzlement, and then fell back into the rhythm of 'Knit one, pearl two'. Not once did I stutter, even when I struggled to sound out a word. With Graybeard's departure, I believed I was exorcised of my stutter.

Mother Brush kept a tight lip on chit-chat of town gossip until the article about Colonel Simon came out. The day I read the criticism of his spending, Mother Brush laid her knitting aside, looked me in the eye and took me into her confidence. She began, "Theophilus, how quickly Xenia forgets! Congress, you know is an elected body of State Representatives and Senators." I learned that in government studies. "Congress is made up of people chosen and elected by Xenia citizens. It was Congress who stopped the Capitol Lawn Easter Egg Roll. They said the grass needed to be protected so they passed the 'TURF LAW'. The law put a cease and desist on Easter Egg Rolls ever after."

"Xenia families take the train to the Capitol's Egg Rolls every year."

"Of course. And it was those same people who got their underwear in a wad when Congress forbid it." I grabbed my mouth and laughed, catching serious Mother Brush off guard. She crinkled her nose and joined the laughter. Both of us held our sides. "I'm sorry, that wasn't a nice thing for me to say." And we laughed more.

"Theophilus, it was Mrs. Rutherford B. Hayes who immediately offered the White House lawn for Egg Rolls. It has been that way ever since. Xenia children kept on rolling eggs and lived happily ever after, due to the kindness of Mrs. Hayes. How soon the citizens forgot." Mother Brush reached for her tea cup and blew on the steaming liquid as she lost herself 'cloud counting', as she called it. I waited, forgotten at her feet until she came out of her clouds of big thoughts. "Mrs. Hayes saved the Egg Roll and she saved the Orphans of the Big War. How dare Xenia criticize our tree planting." Annoyed, she grabbed the paper, folded it and said, "Mrs. Hayes' husband is Republican. This is a Democratic paper." That compartmentalized Mother's thoughts.

Then on a sparkling, blue summer day when the temperature soared into the triple digits, Colonel Simon showed the town he knew what he was doing. He assembled a sun-scorching march to Duck-Butt-Pond. Colonel Simon stepped out in parade march of absolute cadence. "I saved my horse. The bullet did not penetrate my saddle," was all he said about the limp he contracted in the Big War. The cadets rumored that his thigh was so infected the surgeon wanted to amputate his leg and that he hobbled out of the hospital, and his men carried him to a tree where they treated his wound with leeches that ate away the infection. Some cadets said the Colonel was afraid to go to sleep and he sat propped against a tree with a sentry whom he ordered to "Shoot any hacksaw surgeon who comes for my leg."

Colonel Simon circled the cadets on the pond bank, raised his ever-present megaphone. Headless, he commanded, "Gentlemen, make yourselves proficient in the manly art of swimming. Strip down!"

"Yes, Sir." Cadets belly flopped on the pond's ceiling. Curled cadets hit water with the force of discharged cannon balls. Duck-Butt-Pond transformed into a maelstrom of boisterous naked sailors, and man-made waves washed away the heaviness of that lonely Father's Day.

CHAPTER 7: SOUNDS OF SUMMER

James organized his cottage into a Boulder Roll. For one week, cadets put their shoulders to the massive stone left behind when the Ice Age withdrew from Ohio. Boys shoved and coerced the heavy stone across the fields to the pond. There they anchored a jumping off place over Duck-Butt-Pond. James was giving the honor of executing the first dive. To the shouts, my big brother performed a perfect gainer. The applause might have been longer and louder but everyone was pushing and shoving to get a turn on the new diving board. The sound of summer was condensed in bodies slapping against the cooling waters of Duck-Butt-Pond, and it continued until flowers faded and wind withered leaves.

James became a running back and brought the outside world in to Puddin and me. He told us about all the games he played in and we hung on his every word. "O.S.S.O. is undefeated! Other football teams fear us, knowing cadets drill every day and it makes us strong athletes. We memorize marching formations which easily transfer into football plays. Other teams are soft. When we walk on the field we stare fear into our opponents." James laughed and slapped his knee. "The Home Cadets have a reputation that follows us far and wide." He grew serious and dropped his tone, "Puddin, Theo, it is not braggadocio, if you can do it. We can do it." I sucked in air. I was so proud of James and so was Puddin. We went to all the home games where the roar of the crowd when James scored warmed my soul. It was directly proportional: the wetter James' jersey became the louder the crowd cheered. James was the most popular cadet on campus and I wallowed in being his brother.

My pain came with away games. My heart was

gored when James returned melancholy. His head hung and he lowered his voice a decibel and said, "I looked for Old Graybeard." His hurt tore at me and it drove my hatred deeper for the man who hurt my brother. Sport teams were talked about in bars. Papers published game schedules. Papers published game results. Someone, somewhere had told Graybeard about his son's athletics even though the bastard could not read. He could have attended just one of James' games. Damn him.

~ ~ ~ ~ ~ ~

We marched to chapel Saturdays and entered a single door. Quaker-like, we were immediately divided by the aisle. Girls on the right. Boys on the left. If it was Pastor Brock standing on the altar steps, I knew we were in for fire and brimstone. The worn, black fabric of Pastor Brock's coat was shiny with age. Cloth of any color other than black was never worn by Pastor Brock. I wondered if his wife dyed his Long Johns. A tall, bony man with skin stretched to the limits just covered his bones. He had tiny black eyes, held behind round, wire-framed glasses on his too-large head.

"If you wish counsel, fill out a yellow card in the holder in your pew. I will make time for you on my next rotation." That is how he opened his Saturday sermon. No one I ever saw withdrew a yellow card. And no other minister ever offered counsel. "Bow your head for the Lord's Prayer."

Climbing into the pulpit, he bellowed, "Theft!" And grabbed the front edge of the wooden box. "Thievery, Filching, Purloining." He leaned his frame further and further out of the box until he balanced waist high on the edge and glowered down on the left side of the aisle for a breathless minute and then righted himself with dignity, adjusted his suit and pushed back his glasses, a nervous habit repeated throughout his sermons. "It is all the same, all the same." Pastor Brock drove his words into the left aisle harder than a hen pecks sun-baked seeds.

"Cadets walk by Pastor Brock's house and help themselves to apples." He stared and the left aisle seated cadets lowered themselves faster than the snake in the Garden of Eden slid into his den hole. "Filchers who stole all the apples hanging over the fence, returned and brashly entered my yard and purloined apples higher on the tree. You thieves robbed Mrs. Brock of making pies, cobbler and apple sauce. You robbed her as surely as if you held a gun to her head." A congregational gasp floated up from the pews, and Pastor Brock slammed his fist into the pulpit. Cadets fidgeted. They tried to rearrange their faces into a mask of mocked innocence.

"I am in a Den of Thieves." The left aisle stared up at heaven. Their heads became marble carved into unmoving blushes of guilt. "My Good Wife prayed daily for a cadet to knock at her door and politely ask for an apple in the weeks that passed. No knock came. Then one day I returned early to find her crying and wringing her hands. Not because her larder was bare but because of the souls that broke the eighth commandment."

The left side of the aisle continued an upward stare. The right side of the aisle continued a sideways glare. Pastor Brock removed a black handkerchief and wiped frothy, white spittle from his mouth corners. He folded and returned the wet cloth to his pocket and stood sadly shaking his head and catching his breath. "I told my wife to put away her tears, that God sent me to save souls. I removed the seducers. I axed my apple trees."

A liturgical moan was delivered. He leaned over the pulpit and exhaled breath that felt as cold as the air released from Jesus' tomb. "Stand and sing Hymn 203."

~ ~ ~ ~ ~ ~ ~ ~

Duck-Butt-Pond froze. Hours of ice hockey melted into spring and our days were busier than a swarm of bees fanning the Queen. We worked hard preparing for Decoration Day, our holiday. Christmas, Easter and Thanksgiving people stayed in their homes with their families and sent food to the Home and small gifts, but Decoration Day people entered our grounds. Decoration Day Eve held little sleep for us.

Led by a lone, riderless horse with stirrups turned backwards, our parade began. We advanced behind the Grand Army of the Republic, who marched two decades and eight years ago in blue uniforms that were now faded. Onlookers' applause sounded like long ago thundering hooves to the G.A.R. Some limped, some walked with canes, but not one was out of step with our boy drummer. A few of the soldiers rode on a horse-drawn wagon bed.

Our teen girls donned chalk-white dresses with matching large bows at their waists and in their hair. The girls carried bouquets of dew-sprinkled poppies, picked from Puddin's class garden. Younger girls wore wreaths of Baby's Breath. Toddlers wobbled on unsure legs. Their baby fat hands clutched onto an old halyard, a rope retired from its use of raising and lowering the courtyard flag. The rope was anchored on each end by cottage mothers.

Teenage boys shouldered weapons. Younger uniformed lads carried American flags and jabbed at the wind in various versions of their orders to 'wave your flag.'

Lastly cottage mothers paraded prams of infants dressed in white layettes with white ribbon caps tied under their chubby chins. Four baby heads bobbed along the parade route in the corners of each pram until one slid from sight and the mother had to re-prop the infant up on the soft pillow. Occasionally, a cottage mother carried a crying babe whom she swaddled under the shade of her wide millinery.

The parade drew up in a stand of trees behind the chapel. Horses were unhitched and ushered away to a bag of waiting oats. The wagon bed became a stage. Cadets scrambled out of long held formation and rushed to dot every cemetery grave. The boys placed their flags on graves and girls laid their flowers as smiling soldiers and citizens watched. Children took a seat on the grass, and many fell asleep after a sleepless night and a long march. Soldiers who were flung far from their fighting days stood and delivered speeches orated in age-weakened voices. Though the fire of their convictions may be a reduced flame, their bellies held a low-burning ember of the belief that they did the right thing. And that belief shone brightly in their eyes.

General Hewitt, decorated four stars, stood and raised his arms to quiet the crowd. Cottage mothers nudged fidgeting children. Boys picked grass stems and stuck them in their mouth. General Hewitt first off commended the folks for coming to the cemetery and visiting the dead. "I fear the population will forget their graves. Guard them with sacred vigilance," he asked of the gathering.

Everyone stood and sang Battle Hymn of the Republic. Some sang with hands on their hearts. At the ending of the song, a darkened bugler's silhouette blew haunting notes over the cemetery. Taps concluded the ceremony. Old soldiers shook hands and made fragile promises of . . .'Next year'. A promise some could not keep. James traveled among the soldiers mired in grief. He was still searching for the one who went AWOL.

I rushed to join others helping themselves to lemonade and cookies. For every cookie I ate, I fed one to my pocket. Bella Kirkendall, Wand Drill Captain, who snubbed me the day before and the day before that and every day since I came to the Home sidled up to me. Her Wedgewood-blue eyes lowered under a shrub of thick lashes. She pulled her sausage curls aside and pressed her lips against my ear. "Theo, would you carry a cookie for me?"

Charmstruck, my knees knocked each other. Fearing a stutter, I could not answer. I went back to the cookie table, stuffed my pockets while Bella turned her back and pretended she had not sent me on the mission. Under her spell, I followed her like a puppy back to her cottage, hearing and seeing nothing but the jiggling of her lovely sausage-shaped curls. When she stopped under the porch roof, I stepped to her side and she opened her palms. I handed over two fists of cookies, emptying my pockets. Bella took the cookies stepped inside and closed the door on my only thought, "Will she be my friend tomorrow?"

CHAPTER 8: COMMENCEMENT

"Make Cottage 22 proud," Mother Brush ordered daily. We had a half day of instruction and a half day of shop divisible by lunch. Some days, Mother followed her marching children, at a tardy distance. She walked in with one of her charges who stayed in bed faking a fever. "I request his homework be doubled." She deposited the child and left.

Mother Brush visited the infirmary where she read to a tonsillectomy, mumps or measles ill child. Mother was gentle to the ill and harsh on frauds. During 1897, she lived in the Infirmary taking turns sitting beside her children's beds. I remember her reading Classics to the ward. Sometimes she let her knitting needles fly carrying away her anxiety for the sleeping listless child under her watchful eye. She knitted booties for our hands so we could not scratch our measles. She kept a standing order of plenty of pudding for her sick children.

Ohio Soldiers and Sailors Home had nine grades of reading, arithmetic and geography. Penmanship and spelling rode piggyback on one received grade. Work completed to a teacher's satisfaction permitted free time at the classroom globe. The globe was studied carefully, and names were memorized of all the wonderful places cadets wanted to travel.

Today was a very important day. Our cottage was to take the Grade School Exit Exam. One had to make a ninety-five or better for entrance into the high school two-year vocational program. Then followed Commencement.

Cadets always boasted of traveling the globe when they graduated. They wanted to travel for travel's sake. There were only two children who ran away in the years I've been here. And they returned on their own. I don't really count them as runaways. At the Asylum, kids ran daily, sometimes hourly. And no one ever returned on their own. Asylum children were bound in fish net, arms to their sides, and a large collar was placed about their necks to prevent them from spitting on and biting the police or truant officers who returned them.

~ ~ ~ ~ ~ ~

O.S.S.O.'s night watchman, Charles Buckles, entered my life on the cusp of the twenty-first century. I misspoke. I encroached upon his life. Mr. Buckles was what I wished Graybeard could have been for James. James needed Papa. I did not. Ole Puddin Head was a fence-sitter, and sometimes he mentioned the sperm donor I wanted to forget.

Mr. Buckles was Paul Bunyan size in my eyes. Cadets feared the figure who roamed campus veiled in the night, who had the stealth of a panther. Mr. Buckles was the shadow who grabbed offending cadets with a bear-like grip. And he never hesitated to report the offense to Colonel Simon. Not once did an offender talk his way out of a Buckles report. The majority of reports consisted of names of nocturnal visitors beneath a female's raised window. Or a piece of female undergarment thrown into a waiting offender's hands. Misconduct resulted in kitchen duty, mopping floors, peeling potatoes, shelling peas, breaking string beans, carrying out garbage to add to the stench of the compost pile. But worst of all, slopping pigs was bad because they chased you and bit you. If the offense was committed in the winter, offenders were assigned to work the Sugar Camp and cadets hated the work. They hated being under the directions of the 'White Indian'.

I loved Sugar Camp. I loved the slant of the winter sunlight in the woods and walking the winding silver paths of moonlight. I loved the slow-walking, slow-talking night watchman who floated an aura of peacefulness. I happily followed in the noiselessness of Mr. Buckles' snow-crunching, tread-marking foot steps. It was an honor to check sap buckets. "Make sure you hang them, just so," he demonstrated. Buckets not hung properly were emptied by winter's howling wind. Traveling with Mr. Buckles, I saw things I had only heretofore read about. Foxes, skunks and wolves crossed paths with us. Squirrels lay flat on limbs and scolded us in their high-pitched way. Hawks soared overhead and would pluck a trembling field mouse who could not quite find cover.

Proudly, I can say, I never saw my buckets empty of sap. Mr. Buckles and I harvested almost four hundred gallons of sweet semifluid in an all-time high for the season. Some of it was soaked into mush and the rest we sold at Farmer's Market. Mr. Buckles never took a cent from the sales. He donated the entire amount to the Home.

Mother gave me permission to visit Mr. Buckles after dinner when my chores and homework were complete. I went over and stood on his guardhouse threshold most evenings. The guardhouse was built like a rabbit hutch. It was a long windowless room with a slanted roof that met the back wall a yardstick above his desk. It resembled the Greene County Fair's fun house. The desk and Mr. Buckles ate up every inch of the space forcing me to wait on the threshold. He would snort, "What do you want?" Keeping his back to me. After a length of my unanswered silence, he would push off the desk, swivel his chair and face me in mock surprise. "Oh, the thorn in my side. I was afraid it was the Colonel coming to fire me."

Mr. Buckles made me feel free to open any subject for conversation, and I burdened him with heavy and trivial concerns. He responded to both with the same amount of interest. Charles Buckles took time and interest in a boy that society forgot.

One summer's end when the temperature dipped low enough to make you feel winter was rounding the bend, Mr. Buckles turned our routine upside down. This night, he swiveled, faced me and banged out his words faster than a typewriter could ink a page. I was given to think he was angry. Emotions blocked my understanding of the words whizzing by my ears.

"Won't you be assigned a trade this year?"

"Uh, I guess. Sir."

"Theo, you turned up here like a tiny bird blown off course."

"I turned up here because some bastard abandoned me." Mr. Buckles held his counsel in the awkward moment while I readied myself for a lecture on cussing. None came.

"Orphanages are full of children placed in them by an unbearable loss. It took some years for you to get your footing. I was standing in the back of the gymnasium the day you recited total recall of the Nursery Rhyme, Rub-A-Dub-Dub."

Oh gobshite. I had no idea. My face reddened and I wanted the ground to swallow me.

"I figured you must have had a home with some kind of learning, or someone who read to you. Some kids don't. Some kids wander life lost. I don't want that for you. Tonight, you must decide on your trade." He rested his chin on steepled fingers and gave me a wry smile. "You made 100% on your Exit Exam."

"No one told me."

"Tomorrow, they will. I was made aware that you are good at beating irons." His eyebrows questioned me.

"Now you are funning. Right?"

"No. Smithy allows you to work his bellows, right?"

"Smith is a philosopher." I wanted to diminish my role in the livery. "I just hold the horse while Smith shoes and I listen to the stuff he talks about. He talks. I listen. That is all."

"Smith tells me you stroke the horses. You calm them. Isn't that so?"

I wanted to forgo this dissection. "Look, just make your point. Sounds like you and Smithy worked me over pretty good." My words unveiled anger that I did not mean. I was uncomfortable and I was posturing.

"Smith says you don't jump away from sparks. He can pound metal white and you stay right beside him working the bellows. Did you not pound scrap on his anvil?"

"Oh, thunder." I fell deeper into the embarrassment of being discussed. I was a kid. I just wanted to be left alone.

"Smithy told me you can swing and you are good at tickling the heat. His words, exactly."

"Mr. Buckles, Sir. I placed scraps in an open fire. I coaxed them into shapes. I enjoyed playing with metal, but if I might say so you make me feel like a grasshopper being dissected in science class."

The man dug deeper. "Smithy says you grind axes on his grindstone and grinding is a talent, a finesse, God given, not taught."

I countered. "Axes are easy, thin hoe blades I break."

"You make presents?"

I moaned and slid down to my knees. My ears burned under the interrogation. "Stop! Please. Smith saved pieces of scrap and I made them into a simple wind chime for Mother Brush. You know, to ring in the new century. A once in a lifetime occasion, that's all."

"Yes, I saw it hanging outside her reading window. She tells me it is the best gift she ever received, and every time she hears the chimes, she thinks of you."

Joseph, Mary and Jesus. Will the man stop? I could not stop the smile growing on my face as I remembered her opening the gift. She thanked me and kissed the top of my head, just they way Mama kissed me.

"You ain't afraid of me." His words yanked me back from thoughts of Mama. I stared at his ever-present toothpick. Mr. Buckles' tongue chased the toothpick around his mouth. Over and over it rolled the sliver of wood back and forth. "Mule kicked, eh?"

"Almost to the next county. I was ass over appetite."

"Yes, but you got back up, smoothed your hair, soothed the mule and collared her like she was a kitten. Smith's words. True?" I looked away. "You can spread a horse's lips, look at his teeth and give the age within a year. Son, it ain't my intent to embarrass you. I am intent on finding out if you gave any thought to becomin' a blacksmith. A wagon wright."

Nerves undone, I clawed at my head with the rapidity of a tree squirrel. My tongue was lost. My words whirled in a vortex. It was a long time since anyone called me son.

"There is money in broken wagons, wheels and tongues, Theo. Spokes, anvils, ploughshares, they all need fixing. If you are a natural hammer swinger, you have a God-given talent. Smithy says the 'Rhythm of Smithing cannot be taught.' You got the rhythm. I was thinking if you put aside some earnings you stand a chance of setting up your own livery. Be your own boss."

I was dumbstruck. These had never been my thoughts. I was not sure what to say, but I knew it was something I liked to do. I liked the livery. I liked the heat and the smell. I liked the horses and the sassy mules. "Yeah, I might do that."

"Well then you need to make a firmer acquaintance with numbers."

Oh thunder! Ice water formed in my veins. I ground my shoe toe in the dirt, covering my pant legs halfway up with dust. They had spoken. Mr. Buckles discussed me with Mr. Baldasare. Mr. Buckles stepped into the night behind me, leaned against his office and gave me a long hard look. I stopped dredging the dust trench. "You must understand, only in the mastery of numbers does a man keep from being parted from his money."

"Mama taught me numbers. I knew that crap before I came here. I know sums and subtraction. Mr. Baldasare is nothing and he taught me nothing I didn't know." Anger flared. He talked about me to everyone it appears. Whack! Mr. Buckles hit my butt.

"You cussed, boy, and I let that pass, but I will not stand for you calling a 'nothing'. Everyman is important. Mr. Baldasare taught you nothing because you accepted nothing. He called it not applying yourself. I call it 'muleheaded'. You came into his class riding math skills way ahead of your years. For that you ought to get down on your knees and thank your Mama. Pride held you up but you fell behind because you did not apply yourself. Know-it-all you did not take arithmetic seriously. Theo, you failed to increase knowledge in the wonderful basics your Mama provided for you. And you stand before me with no shame."

Tears stung my eyes. I had let Mama down. She would be ashamed I hadn't grasped opportunity. I ground my shoe deeper in the dust. Mr. Buckles laid his large hand on my shoulder and squeezed. "Make your arithmetic book your best friend. Make your Mama proud. This isn't the Boy's Academy, but it is an education being offered just the same." He pulled me into a hug. I sobbed in uncontrollable heartache. I sobbed long-held tears. When his shirt was completely soaked he said, "A man cannot run a business, figure labor and materials without good math skills. You are being handed the chance to make your Mama proud by becoming a 'Toiler of the Forge'." I looked up and promised to follow the path.

"Theo, don't waste your life cursing the man who sired you. Your story isn't over. It has just begun and you might find the man did you a favor."

~ ~ ~ ~ ~ ~

Summer break scattered cadets. Lawrence was going to visit his mother in Xenia. Ralph's grandfather sent him a train ticket to Goes Station, first stop out of Yellow Springs. There Ralph would work on his family farm where he complained the work was hard. Then he erased my sympathy in a single sentence. "On Sundays, Grandpa and I dip wet lines in the Little Miami River and eat a picnic lunch. Sunday night dinner is always a Fish Fry."

Sullen, I asked. "Could he use another pair of hands?" I never got an invite. And I never tortured myself listening to his return stories about the farm.

Some older cadets got summer jobs at Yellow Springs Hotel. A hotel wagoner collected them where the Home's entrance met the street, saying he didn't want to turn his team around in our driveway. That job provided James and all the boys with the finest dining. They served the food and ate the food of the same chef. James bronzed up on off-hours by diving from the limestone cliffs into cold bubbling, peach-colored waters. James said they dove looking for a caboose believed to have wrecked and fallen to the bottom of the water hole. James carried luggage, mailed visitors packages, postcards and letters, which provided him with great stories and great tips. Tip money was his favorite way to size up a person. James had a way with people and the hotel was glad to have him.

The O.S.S.O. summer picnic was held for remaining cadets on the campus. They numbered in the majority. There were years when June's picnic was rained out and our spirits were muddied. If July was cancelled we fell further down-in-the-mouth. August could be counted on to blaze hot and hold our picnic but the wait seemed eternal. But always the eve of the picnic came and I was sleepless. Morning of the picnic we all left the dining hall at fire drill speed and ran to the gymnasium where girls plucked bean bags and jump ropes and boys grabbed baseballs and bats.

Clifton residents, Captain and Mrs. Dohme, sponsored the commemoration of their only child who died in infancy. And they certainly gave the picnic a lot of forethought. The spread-together began with a kettle of butter beans and black-eyed peas and another kettle of creamed barley soup set on a tree stump. We were allowed to ladle all day. This was something not allowed on the other 364 days of the year. Men carried in a roasted pig from which we pulled pork off, at whim, the live-long day. Platters of red and green tomatoes, potato salad, pickled carrots and coleslaw rested under tents of white netting. Honey infused Spoon Bread replaced our usual fare of biscuits. I decorated my bread in different colors of homemade preserves. No one touched the apple butter. In fact the taste for apple anything had left most everyone's tongue. I ate gingerbread and blackberry cobbler until my stomach was rock hard.

Everyone ate, played and ate again. We tried to tie the sun in the sky that day, to delay sunset. An hour before the sun did slip from view, Captain Dohme brought out thick cream, salt and ice along with a churn. We took turns slapping the mixture. "Paddle the mixture twice around and do-si-do the middle." He said. Our work brought us ice cream.

"Oatmeal Hermits," Mrs. Dohme announced, unveiling the basket of cookies made of rolled oats, flour, butter and sugar filled with sweet meats. Cadets lay littered across the ground, held down by heavy, paperweight stomachs. We lost our grip on the sun and it floated over the horizon. A bonfire was lit.

CHAPTER 9: FAMILY REQUESTED DISCHARGES

Family requested discharges tore our cottage family asunder. Albert, tall for his age, was our first requested discharge. Parents who would not provide for their children waited until the child could work, and then requested the child be discharged to the family. A child added back into the family when he became an asset, as another income. Mother Brush saw it many times over but she covered her sorrow with happy chatter for the child's sake. Unsuspecting children were so happy to be going home. Albert went to live with his father.

Shortly after Albert's departure, Mrs. Brush bumped into Albert's aunt coming out of Canon's Candy Shop on South Detroit Street. His aunt said that Albert's father moved to Wellston, Ohio, and Albert went to work at Buckeye Furnace. Then she unloaded, "That nothing-of-a-man waited on Albert's first pay day, bragging about being first in line. When the pay window opened, he laid claim to the boy's pay before Albert crawled out of the coal mine. Then the jobless man drank up his motherless son's paycheck. The entire time Albert was waiting at home in a house with an empty pantry. I begged my brother-in-law to let me keep Albert, but he already had his scheme and the low-life refused me. I wish he died instead of my sainted sister." She took out her handkerchief and blew her nose and wiped her tears. Mrs. Brush patted her arm.

Mother Brush grieved deeply for Albert until the day she received a postcard. She showed us that the card was signed, 'Albert'. Nothing more. Her finger pointed out the cancelled postmark, which we had not noticed. 'Mesa, Arizona'. With that she tucked the card in her Bible where she kept others. That ended Mother's grieving. Her little bird had flown.

Mother Brush was shopping for thread in town when she met Mrs. Kirkendall, Bella's mother. Mrs. Kirkendall had produced a family requested discharge for Bella. "I set her up in the formal parlor. I hung an oversized pink painted sign and stenciled it in the most beautiful shade of forest green. It hangs over the front porch steps. Have you seen it?"

Mother Brush shook her head. She made it a practice of not going near her children's homes after they left her care. It would be too painful.

"You must come by. The sign advertises sewing, wedding gowns, dresses, layettes, embroidery, alterations and patchwork. I do a little bit of patchwork, but customers in need of patchwork are too poor usually to pay to have it done. Most of our work is for new clothes. Rich women will occasionally have alterations done, but most of the time it is work done from scratch. A dozen customers filled our parlor the first day. Well, it was nice to see you. Goodbye."

Mrs. Brush called to the woman's back. "Give Bella our regards." Bella's House Mother shared Bella's poignant letters with Mrs. Brush. They were written on paper discolored by heat of a nearness to her oil lamp. Bella lamented that her eyesight had dimmed rapidly, and her Mrs. Kirkendall refused to divert profits for the sake of buying her spectacles. Bella said she was beaten 'savagely' was the word she used. If a customer complained of the gaps in the stitching, she was beat. If a customer complained the customer candy dish was empty, Bella was beat. Bella wrote that she was screamed at if dust accumulated on the top of her sewing box.

The day I inquired if Mrs. Brush had heard anything from Bella's Cottage Mother she told me Bella's letters had stopped.

"Someday I will find Bella and marry her." I swore to myself and Mrs. Brush.

~ ~ ~ ~ ~ ~

My time at the Home was just about over. As we neared graduation, cadets boasted about travels. "I'll see the world. I'll drink the night away. I'll have a woman on each arm." It was all blatherskite and I was a blatherskite too. I talked of traveling to Cairo and Amsterdam, but unlike the others, I was lying. Mama said, "The cruelest lies are the ones you tell yourself. Those damage your soul."

One night, I sat crying under a large, oak tree and Cadet Roscoe Yarborough veered off the sidewalk, crossed the grass heading straight for me. I stifled sobs into soft hiccups. Time at O.S.S.O. Roscoe had grown into a solid, broad-shouldered man with a large face and a full mustache. He swaggered with confidence I never owned. I was in awe of his physique. We all were. Over the past few weeks, Roscoe showed us letters of promised jobs he had lined up and only needed to make a decision. He quoted salaries and work hours of these jobs. I had no doubt Roscoe would make it on the outside. I had every doubt about myself. "Don't cry," he told me and sat down. "Won't be long, Theo. We short-timers feel we can't make it across the finish line, but we can. And all the world is waiting. Look at James. He did it. Maybe you can go to California where he is. Chin up." He slapped my knee and walked off never knowing I cried because I did not want to leave. All the lies I told in the circle of crowing cadets damaged my soul. I just wanted to find Bella, bring her back here and marry her. She and I could become Cottage parents like Mrs. Brush and her late husband.

~ ~ ~ ~ ~ ~

Puddin graduated two years ago. He switched from Agriculture to Telegraphy and it landed him a good job at the Dayton Telegraph Office. He sent me a Christmas note the first Christmas he was out, but he never wrote again. I kept telling myself that he could not take a day off work, lose wages for his little brother's commencement. James graduated five long years ago and I miss him. He rode the rails out of Xenia and through Dayton and never stopped at Graybeard's house. James left with a barber's license under his belt. Tim Brock graduated with James, and he came back to campus and said he had been in California and stopped at James' barbershop. He said James sent word to me that he was fine, married and owned his own shop. I visioned him many a night 'holding court and cutting hair'. James was a magnet. He attracted people.

"Theophilus Kabel," I crossed the stage under the raucous whistling of a man standing in the back of the folding chairs. He wore a string tie and flattened his hair with corn oil that glistened. I did not know him. Mr. Baldasare, diploma purveyor, shook my hand and said, "Fine job. Good luck to you." I nodded, took my diploma, shook his hand and stumbled past him catching myself before falling head first off the side stage steps.

"Could you eat some cookies?" It was Mr. Buckles. He had moved up from the back and met me at the steps.

"No, Sir." I laughed. "I didn't recognize you." We walked to the edge of the crowd.

"Congratulations. You did it." We moved further away from the back slappers to a large oak tree. I watched his eyes drift up the tree that shaded the commencement party. "There was an old owl, lived in this oak and the more he heard, the less he spoke."

I chimed in. "The less he spoke, the more he heard." We chorused, "Oh if men were all like that wise old bird." Mr. Buckles threw back his head and laughed heartily. A sight I had never seen. "Mrs. Armstrong's English class?"

He laughed harder, "No, my mother's knee."

I looked up at the tree. "I bet a thousand cadets climbed every forbidden limb of that old oak." He and I knew tree climbing was forbidden by Colonel Simon after several broken arms had been set.

"Only after a thousand Shawnee and Miami children climbed that oak. Xenia closed in on a path first trampled by buffalo hooves. Bull Skin Trace the Indians called it. It led north from the Ohio River and cut through what is now the center of town. People always begin history with themselves." He smiled and sat down on the ground, cross-legged. "Cadets replaced Indian children, Theo, on those tree limbs. Barefooted children ran over this soil and swam in your pond." He removed his string tie. "I have suffered long enough for you."

My eyes focused on a bump under his shirt. "Cadets say you are an Indian." I was startled at my own brashness and wanted to take my words back. A tiny smile broke his face and he measured me in silence.

"What do you think?"

Jesus, Joseph and Mary. "Forgive me, please. I did not learn from that wise old owl." The heat of my Irish blood turned me 'rua faced', as Mama called my blush.

Mr. Buckles' hand went deep in his shirt and he pulled out something on a thin leather necklace and dangled it gently between us. "Because of this?" I swallowed hard. My eyes averted him. I wanted to bury myself in a rabbit's warren. "Look." he demanded.

I raised my eyes. "I am so sorry. I've ruined our day. Please don't be angry with me." Tears salted my cheeks.

"It isn't our day, Theo. It is our last day! Now look at me." A deer hoof lay in his open palm. He was silent as smoke while he rolled the hoof between his thumb and index finger. Panic squeezed my throat. A cold sweat bathed me. I waited. "Indians wear deer hooves as a symbol to keep themselves gentle, like the deer. A hoof is a reminder to keep peace foremost in your mind. My grandfather, a great Indian Scout, spoke the language of many tribes. He was the bravest man I ever knew and he was the most gentle. His gentle heart was pierced by an angry man's arrow. My grandfather had sworn to my grandmother if he was ever wounded and he could jump in a river. He would just to save his scalp. He believed the lowest form of insult was to lose one's scalp. And that is what he did. He jumped in the Mad River. I walked downstream until I found him or what was left of his body caught on a fallen log. I buried him and returned his hoof to my grandmother. She placed it at her breast, keened one week for him, and at the end of that time, she handed the hoof to me and asked I wear it all my earth days. I keep that promise, daily."

"It worked, for you are the most gentle man I know."

"It wasn't always so, Theo. I found my grandmother caught in quicksand. She was there trying to hide from being forced out of Ohio at the time of the Indian cleansing." He stopped, put the hoof back inside his shirt. "Let's keep them guessing. Pact?"

"Pact." He shook my left hand, Indian fashion.

We sat side by side in the growing twilight. "Theo, when I was in school and felt it was time to graduate, I graduated myself and leaped the windowsill of the second grade." His eyes flashed and then grew sad. I left him alone in his thoughts. A mosquito buzzed his ear and he swatted it. "I lacked the Mother Wit to know what I was doing. Still in knee britches, I made a choice that turned me into a solitary, nocturnal wandering sentry. Night's blackness has been my only friend. It is not good and I do not wish the same for you, Son." I flung myself into him and we fell backwards on the grass.

"I'll write."

He scoffed. "If you wish. That would be nice, but I won't write back!" We straightened ourselves. I saw his grimace. "Neither can I write forward." I did not laugh at his joke. Embarrassed, he hung his head. "But I can read. Yes, I can and I promise to read every word you write. I'll save all your mailings, Theo." He stood and looked over the partiers. A sorrowful silence stood between us. People were clearing tables and folding chairs. I delayed my departure until he handed me my tiny bag of belongings, a comb, a toothbrush, a pocket Bible which was a gift from Pastor Brock. My tin cup engraved T.K. a gift from Smithy. All my possessions lay on top of Puddin's well-worn Christmas card.

"I see kids come in here hating this place and then grow to depend on the boundaries until a fear of stepping outside the boundary grows so big in them they isolate themselves in boarding rooms somewhere, afraid to venture into the free world. It is what I call institutionalized. I don't want that for you. Theo, even an ocean has a strand, a boundary, but it does not keep it from lapping at the shore. You are smart and you have a lot to give the world. I am glad to see you go. I want the best in life for you." His voice broke. I stood.

"Oh, I almost forgot." Reaching in his pocket he pulled out a twenty-dollar bill. "This will help you towards a set of blacksmith tools. I don't know the cost of tongs, but maybe you can buy an anvil or a used forge. Smith said to get the dealer to throw in bellows on the deal. I don't know . . . " Tears rinsed away his words.

"Thank you." I blubbered and put the money in my pocket.

"Knock it off." His eyes snapped. He wrapped his massive arms around me and squeezed breath from my lungs, making me cough. Then he lifted me off the ground until my toes dangled. I wheezed and slid out of his arms, then walked away from the man I loved more than any other person. I would have given the money back if I could have bought another hour of his time. After I reached the length of the driveway, I turned at the entrance posts and looked back. He was still there.

CHAPTER 10: NEWCOM PLACE

Father Osterday lifted the baby boy up for the eyes of the congregation. Stained glass windows brought a halo upon the infant's Irish ginger curls. "Theophilus Kabel Junior," The white robed priest announced from where he stood on the altar steps. Beside the priest stood the godparents of the baptized babe, Mr. and Mrs. Charles Buckles. Mrs. Buckles-former-Mrs. Brush led the applause. The little boy gleefully smiled at the congregation. His baptismal dress radiated in prisms of stained window glass color that wrapped him in a rainbow of God's making.

After church, the Kabels invited Father Osterday and the Buckles back to the house for dinner. They broke bread at the happy occasion, and toasts were made to the guest of honor who slept through most of the party. The Buckles shared stories about Theo Senior's days at O.S.S.O. "Sounds like you had two four-eyes watching over you." Father Osterday said as he shook Theo's hand and thanked him for the lovely dinner.

"I did." Theo answered unabashedly.

The Buckles thanked Theo and his wife, Lola, for allowing them the privilege of becoming godparents. "We are honored." Mrs. Buckles kissed the sleeping baby goodbye and she and Charles caught the train to the Home where they were employed as Cottage Parents. Mr. Buckles retired from night watchman and joined his wife in parenting a ready-made family of sons. After visiting with Theo and Lola they were convinced he was happy and the hole in his heart was healed.

~ ~ ~ ~ ~ ~

A week later winds peeled back the corner of March. Father Osterday, a copy of Friar Tuck, stood between two policemen on the fringes of falling rain. He knocked on the door, and Lola opened it to them. Her tired eyes took on the trio and she stepped back not speaking. Her housecoat was stained and wrinkled, and her engorged breasts of unused milk stretched her buttonholes into large gaps. Her hair was twisted into a rat's nest of gnarls and she looked at the men through red eyes. Then she scurried down the hall behind her retreating to kitchen whispering.

A shaft of light floated through a worn spot of the drawn curtain. Dust motes spiraled downward to the floor. A rocking chair squeaked in a slow rhythm in the darkened room. Over in the corner a ghost of a man rocked. Father Osterday could not believe it was the man he had been with in this house the week before. Bereft of time, the grandfather clock stood in the corner with hands clutched at ten. The long, gold pendulum dangled motionlessly behind the clock's glass door. Mirrors were draped and all pictures faced the wall. The Man-of-God moved toward the rocking chair, while the patrolmen scanned the room for a rifle, maybe leaning against a wall or a gun lying on a table. No weapons were seen.

Father laid a hand on Theophilus' shoulder. Theo rocked his son who was dressed in his long, white baptismal gown. A knitted white cap covered the little boy's head, and it was tied with a satin bow under his fat chin. A drooling bib rested on the baby's unmoving chest. He was swaddled in a white blanket and laid on a white satin pillow. He was dead. "Theophilus, it is time."

A wrenching sob pierced the cloistered room. "Father, why couldn't it have been me?"

"I don't know, Son, but you need to be strong now for Lola."

"That son-of-a-bitch undertaker is rushing us. Isn't

he? He wants my son in the ground so he can be home in time for supper. The gobshite! I'd like to knock him in the bollocks."

The police moved toward the raver. Father Osterday shook his head. "Stop with the swearing. This is a priest." Sergeant Derby whispered and nudged Theophilus. "Have you forgotten your manners?"

Father knelt beside the rocker. He softened his voice. "Theophilus, grave-side services are mandatory in this case. The circumstances and all with your baby."

Theo growled through bared teeth. "He has a name." Then his voice rose and he screamed in the priest's face. "My son has a name!"

Sergeant Derby stepped to the other side of the rocker. He wanted to knock the man, but what could you do with a man rocking his dead baby? What?

"Forgive me. I am sorry. Yes, Theophilus Junior is a beautiful baby. And . . ." Theo cut off the priest. "Screw time. Screw the undertaker. And screw this frecking city with its laws."

"It was not Undertaker Murray's decision, Theo." Father stood. "You understand why there can be no wake."

"Bedamn if I can! I don't understand. And what the hell are cops doing here? Someone shut up those kitchen whisperers. All of you can go to hell. There is not one sick bastard in this house, Father. Is there? Tell me, do you see one? Hell no! Standing silently through the tirade. Well, what the hell are you waiting for? Answer me. Show me one sick person. You can't do it. Not one person is sick and this house is not quarantined. No doctor posted no damn quarantine sign on the door. Did he?"

Father Osterday stood motionless. The policemen circled the rocker. Father quieted his words to a lullaby level. "City law states a wake may not be held if the cause of death is in question. A three-day wake might cause an epidemic. . ."

"Might bring? Might? That is cockamamie! It is gobshite. And a smart man like you Father knows it."

Father Osterday leaned over and made the sign of the cross on baby Theo's forehead. "Come on, Theo. Let's get your baby to his Heavenly Father."

Theo, Senior looked shocked. His anger did not die easily but his tone did. "Father, other people have three-day wakes. I get nothing. And you know what, I don't give a damn if the entire city dies. Can they die of 'Probable Cause'? Hell no. That is what Theo Junior's death certificate states, Probable . . . Scarlet Fever. I tore it up. Probable my bollocks." Theo paced around the circle of policemen carrying his son. He threw open the front door and walked out. The very round, black-cloaked priest waved off the police and scurried to catch up to Theo.

"You are doing the right thing," he said taking his place beside the grieving man. The kitchen whisperers felt the cold air blow in the open door, and they hurried on their coats and followed. Theophilus Junior's six-year-old cousin pulled an empty pine box on a sled at the end of the little cortege. The two policemen closed the door and returned down the street to headquarters. One buckled his open holster.

The mourners filed two-by-two up Dayton Hill and turned right on Wyoming Street. Along the way people respectfully stepped off the sidewalk. Men removed their hats and women placed a hand over their hearts. Little children stared. Residents pulled curtains aside keeping a hidden watch on the sad little procession, but their stares were felt. One woman dressed in black stepped off the sidewalk and held up a crucifix. She said. "Blessed are they that mourn."

"Curse you, I am not blessed." Theo snarled at her. His mind had only one thought, and like a phonograph needle stuck in a grove it repeated, "Why God? Why God?"

Four obelisks stood guard at the cemetery entrance.

Strangely the stone pinnacles brought Theo peace. He did feel as if he had brought his baby to the Heavenly Father. He was carrying him into the pearly gates. "Dear God, you know the grace of which I stand most in need."

Ahead, Father Osterday's labored breath of soft grunts on the steep winding switchback brick road could be heard as Father tried to hurry. Theo decelerated feeling no need to rush now and Father pushed ahead. When Theo reached the top of the hill, he saw W. R. Murray, of Murray Funeral Home, standing ankle deep in Baby Land headstones. The sight of the undertaker brought forth a guttural sound that rolled back down the hill. People on Wyoming Street porches looked upwards at Woodland Cemetery.

White lightning flashed from Theo's eyes as he locked on Mr. Murray. "No one touches my son," he laid a charged threat. The undertaker moved crab-like and cowered behind a tree. Father began.

"In the name of the Father, Son and Holy. . ."

"Father," kitchen whisperers screamed. Father Osterday stopped and opened his eyes. Theo stood before the coffin with a raised knife. Unflappable, the priest moved from the head of the coffin to Theo's side just as Theo brought the knife down near the rim of his son's christening cap. Curls fell into his hand. He placed the curls in his pockets. Father Osterday breathed and then restarted the services.

"Amen." Theo kissed every dimpled knuckle on the back of the baby's hand and he pressed each hand against his chest over his heart. He pulled a rattle he forged in the livery and laid it in the baby's grasp then placed him in the coffin and put the lid over the child. "Might I borrow your hammer?" Theo asked the groundskeeper.

"I'll do that for you, Mr. Kabel. I'll take care of everything," he demurred.

Father Osterday dipped his chin at the groundskeeper who was a seven-o'clock, third row sitting Sacred Heart parishioner. The man ceded his hammer to Theo. Theo pounded the first nail, stopped and checked the lid and pulled another nail from his mouth. A circumference of nails, forged by Theo, held the lid in place. Then he began on the second ring of nails. Shivering kitchen whisperers dispersed. Theo wished them begone. He finished the second border of nails and ran his hand lovingly over the lid. "Go my son. You are released from life's pain." Father Osterday blinked back tears. He was reminded of his mother saying people ought to cry when a babe is born and laugh when they die because they are going to a better place.

"I'll leave you now, Theo." The two embraced.

"I'll finish up." The groundskeeper moved forward.

"No. It is my job." Theo's voice was brittle. The groundskeeper handed over the shovel he held and Theo began to shovel dirt. Gently he placed it into the hole. No dirt was thrown. It was all gently laid on the casket. Stones were hand picked from the dirt entering Theophilus Junior's bed. With the last shovel full given, Theo sobbed. "Happy birthday." The baby was twenty-eight days shy of his first birthday.

Copious tears streamed the groundskeeper's face. He took back his shovel and said, "I was there. I saw him baptized, a beautiful lad, that he was. My missus said so too." The Irish brogue of his words touched Theo, and he touched the man's shoulder unable to speak. The groundskeeper reached back in his pocket. Theo took a draw on the proffered flask. "I'll be leavin' you in private."

Theo prostrated himself in abject humiliation in the same way Daniel flattened himself before Gabriel. Positioned on the dirt mound, he prayed the night away under an afghan of snow. When morning broke, Theo cursed God for still being alive. He rocked back up on his knees, pressed on the mound of dirt and smiled for he had kept the baby's dirt warm. "Go find Grand Ma'ma. She awaits you."

CHAPTER 11: OCTOBER TRIAL

Autumn rolled summer's lush, green leaves into tiny brittle parchment scrolls. Ever so slowly, autumn robbed me of shade on my walk between jail and the courthouse. Ankle chains diced my walk into three-hundred and fifty-eight hobbled steps. If not for my accompanying guard, I would look to be a docent, keeping regular working hours as a courthouse tour guide.

My trial was held in an imposing Greek architecture of white limestone extracted from Beavertown Quarry. A little train, Who-Thought-He-Could, brought the stone down Wilmington Avenue on special tracks laid down for just that purpose. Stonecutters with extraordinary skills cut a beautiful flying, spiral staircase. And citizens who entered the massive iron doors traversed a limestone floor which echoed their own footsteps into a feeling of importance not experienced on a wood floor. Citizens straightened their backs, walked with new esteem as they set about their business. Graybeard made not a footstep inside the courthouse during my trial. It was insignificant to him. Puddin George showed no interest. I wonder if California James ever read about the trial in his papers. But then my trial held no appeal to me. I stacked my hands into a pillow and slept.

Deputy Wilson Rice, a large barrel-chested man on pencil thin legs, met me the first day, cuffed and chained me and delivered me to court. I knew I figured him out immediately, and I let him time to figure out me. A deputy has only one conundrum. It did not take him long. His relaxed demeanor told me, he figured out the puzzle. That I was a prisoner with no desire for a footrace was the end of his problem.

Returning to the jail, Rice blabbered. "You sure

know how to draw a crowd. Every inch of space was shoulder to shoulder, Standing Room Only. The upstairs gallery stood three deep and a few looked fixin' to fall over the railing. In all my court watching days, I ain't never seen such a large crowd. Nope, not on the first day."

I kept my head down and counted my steps.

"Trial interest builds, slow-like. The way a kettle comes to a boil. Water gurgles a whisper, roils and breaks into a piercing scream. But by God, you brought them in the first day! There were more people crammed in that court than on the first day of circus entrants under the Fairgrounds Hill Big Top." Rice reached out and patted my back. I jerked away from his touch.

"Don't you lay a hand on me. I ain't your friend, Peckerwood." My voice went up in uncontrollable decibels. I wanted to rain pitchforks on Deputy Rice and the gallery, roosting vultures. "Pecking away at a man's most private moments, you and all those people in there. Feasting on dead carcass. Preying birds, you and them, eating off a dead man's life. If you people had your way, I'd be already swinging out on West Third Street from the river bank, hanging tree." I reined myself in as suddenly as I started and I changed the topic. "Know how many paces lie between the back doors of the jail and courthouse?"

It completely threw Rice. Feelings hurt at my lack of pride in the attendance, he groused. "How the hell would I know and why would I care?"

For the first time, I looked in Rice's eyes. "Because you walk a man between a life and death decision. You walk a decision's width on the life or death of a man."

Rice tried to pick up speed, but the demand of our two-by-two, ark walk, kept him at my side. He could not escape. I began again. "Deputy Rice, that gallery has committed more crimes than all the men held in all the jails in the country. Those pious citizens have cheated in horseflesh sales, robbed neighbor's gardens on moonless nights and have cuckold the ones they sit beside on Sunday church pews. Men in that gallery have refused dying in-laws a sip of water because the bedridden dared linger long after the doctor's predicted date the disease would release their wills. And those gallery bastards beat babies in cribs for soiling themselves. That gallery holds people who beat a hungry orphan who sneaked an extra helping of bread. And they have pocketed food stolen from the people who pay their wages. How do children come to orphanages, if not by abandoning parents or relatives? They are railing-toe-holders, vultures. And some of those stinking spectators will make up my jury. Jury of peers, my bollocks." I threw back my head and howled like a fiend at the sun.

The following day, with much afterthought, Deputy Rice met me with a neighborly air. Henceforth, we did not tromp on each other's lawn, so to speak. We did not talk about the past. We did not talk about the weather nor did we talk about the spectator gallery. We soldered our conversation in the sale of Jim Thorpe from our favorite team, Cincinnati Red Stockings. Thorpe was sold back to the New York Giants and our talk was about the upcoming World Series. Although Rice and I were not Giant fans we spliced together our White Sox boos because of our admiration for Jim Thorpe. Each day we challenged each other with knowledge.

"Jim was a twin." Rice opened.

"I know." I dealt. "The twin died when the boys were eight." And it trumped him. He had no knowledge of that fact.

He came back. "It was a sin to strip him of his Olympic gold." I agreed. Rice raised me. "He accepted money from a team where he played in the off season."

I feigned ignorance then played my singleton. "North Carolina, that was the team." I heard his breath leave his body. The balloon was deflated. "He was either stupid or naive."

"No, he was broke. He took the five dollars." Rice grinned at his lame joke and moved deeper into the game. "Everyone is aware that off-season players take an assumed name."

I nodded. Here goes my ace. "Once I saw a team made up of nine 'John Smiths'." Rice's eyes widened. "Go fish." I amended. The courthouse door stopped our game. On our return trip I opened, "Indian blood won him his gold. His mother was a blend of Sac and Fox Nation." Rice looked up at the sky. I counted my steps. We reached the jail and stepped inside. I waited for him to release my ankle chains.

"Jim played a lot of different sports in school." He panted his words over my chains.

"Basketball, football and baseball." I played my hand.

Rice refused it. "No, not the sports, the name of the school." I had no wild card, no clue. I didn't know.

"Industrial school," he blurted. "His father sent him away saying he could no longer control Jim."

"Gobshite! That isn't a name of a school."

"Ok, Indian Industrial School." He laughed and declared, "Gin." He released my cuffs. I sneered. "Oh well, it was probably best. Jim turned out well."

I looked at him with disgust. "Institutions are filled with people removed from their family, and it is never a good thing to remove a child from his home. It only looks like he turned out well." I was hot and Rice was on alert. "Is he an alcoholic?"

Rice stared at the ground, stiffened and answered. "Is making two hundred and fifty dollars a game, not turning out well?"

"Juda priest," I conceded. "Point Scored." And went to my cell.

The next morning, Rice came for me. We went outside and I filled my lungs with fresh air. "Thorpe's father was Irish-Catholic."

Rice grinned from ear to ear. "No points! I knew that." The shadow of his hand rose to slap my back, hesitated and fell away. We walked on, yoked in our Irish-Catholic footsteps. The sun slid out from behind a flat, gray cloud, and Rice said, "Guess that makes you and I more alike than different." I dropped the subject and the game. It was extremely dangerous to bridge a friendship between a man and his turn-key.

~ ~ ~ ~ ~ ~

"All rise for the Honorable Judge Ulysses S. Grant. Montgomery County Court is now in session."

Lily Grant, the Judge's mother, wedged her maiden name, Simon, between her son's Christian and surname. Lily's husband, Colonel John Grant, fought under General U. S. Grant in the Big War. The Colonel led others to the unspoken conclusion he and the General were related. By the Muses, or the Colonel's prodding, he grew into his name. The fact he was an only child contributed to his ego. Now his refined mother taught him manners and etiquette, but his father trained him bluster and arrogance. The Grants were well known in Vandalia. A Revolutionary Grant, soldier came to Vandalia and spawned them. Three generations of Grants sprouted from the old soldier's seed in Vandalia. "A nothing town," Graybeard declared.

Graybeard's father dug the Miami-Erie ditch across several counties, threw down his shovel and opened an Inn on the edge of the canal waters in Tippecanoe. And the man did it all in the time it took him to sire six sons. The fact that Vandalia was a conduit for the First Federal Road was not important to Graybeard. If a town held no canal they considered it worthless.

U. S. Grant grew into his name and became a powerful attorney and moved to Dayton where his power rose as easily as his bluish cigar smoke. A few years passed and he became a judge. He was dogmatic in thought and left no doubt about who was in charge in his chamber. However on his way to the top he earned a sullied name of 'Cock-of-the-Court'. Judge Grant sported a topknot as white as the hottest part of the flame, and his hair held all the thickness of youth. He strutted Dayton streets with an over-inflated ego and a blunderbuss mouth with a hair-trigger temper. In court he made an august magistrate in his black robe and white hair. It was juxtaposition to his outside antics of being the most colorful figure in town. He was known to keep company with Dayton's madams and Dayton's rogues.

Judge Grant entered his courtroom with an agenda. His black eyes blazed as he kicked his hem across the room, violently pushing his robe out of the way until he made it to his throne. The bailiff stood stiffly beside the elevated desk with eyes lowered to the floor waiting for 'His Honor' to peruse his chamber. U. S. Grant focused first on the main floor, moving his lips as he silently counted. "Ten." He was satisfied. Law permitted just ten women to attend a trial from the main floor. "Women are weak and I will not stop trial for a fainting or hysteria brought on by the showing of an exhibit." That said, Judge Grant slammed the hammer on the law and it was passed, sealed and signed. 'No more than ten women law'.

Secondly, His Honor turned to the upstairs gallery spectators. The intensity of his eyes could wrest a soul to cry out, "Not guilty," even if the person was not on trial. Onlookers shrank from the railing moving back against the crowd as his Judgeship stared upwards. His hawkish eyes took in every face in the room, but mine.

"You may take your seats," the bailiff ordered. I did not hear him. I was reading a sign that hung on the wall, just off to the right shoulder of His 'Highass' when my counsel shoved me down into my chair as hard as Walrus slammed me into the pine board for my first hair cut. My fingers folded into fists and my stomach heaved. I pushed off my chair and sprang up meeting the Public Defender eye to eye. Like a mouser, Rice sprang to his feet and took a waiting step toward me. A curtain of silence dropped on the seated people in the room. I warned him. "Don't ever touch me again, you Nelly."

We sat. I turned back to the sign that hung between the Stars and Stripes and the State of Ohio's pennant-shaped flag. It stated, "Any person caught throwing cigarette or cigar butts, chaws of tobacco in this court will be immediately fined." My, oh my, I wondered, can his 'Highass' fine himself?

~ ~ ~ ~ ~ ~

The selection and swearing in of the jury were over when the Public Defender worked me with a poke. His 'Highass' was addressing the thirteen with the same all-inclusive smile he wore when he bought a round for the house. "Gentlemen, the defendant, Theophilus Kabel, has been arraigned and has entered a plea of 'Not Guilty, Reason Insanity'. He has thrown himself upon God and his country." Not unlike the showman, he raised his arms wide, preacher-like. This was his house, and U. S. Grant embraced the jury as such. Controlled, he returned a smile with the warmth of his gesture. "Remember your oath." The actor-in-him paused producing a somber moment for all smiles to fall away. Bending forward, as if to exclude the onlookers, he held the jury with his eyes, lowered his voice and added, "If, at the end of the trial, you find Mr. Kabel guilty, vote thus."

The jury nodded. He sat back on his throne and tersely, unemotionally described the law. He wasted no words and glided over results he did not expect the jury to return. "Murder done under the influence of passion, the jury may find the defendant guilty of manslaughter. Should it be proved the act was done in self defense, you may find him not guilty." Phlegm of a not guilty verdict coagulated in his windpipe and he cleared his throat. He concluded with a smile that slid from the folds of his eyes and fell off his face like butter slides off a hot knife. His eyes remained cold. "Carry not a word from my chambers or . . ." The threat was dropped in the jury laps, and he sat back to listen and spit his chaw, snuggled cheek.

I laid my head down and dozed off to my landlady's shrill voice description of me. "Theo had a wild look about him."

~ ~ ~ ~ ~ ~

I dreamed I was back on the canal ice-skating. After I left O.S.S.O. I moved to Dayton and got a job at Brown's livery. After work those of us who didn't have to be home for a mother's dinner went ice-skating on the canal and river. Those places were a hotspot of young people, bonfires and laughter. I began two important relationships on the frozen canal. Lola, I met where the canal flowed passed Triangle Park. We began keeping company at the Park's Dance Hall that overlooked the junction of the Stillwater and Great Miami Rivers.

Robert Grant and I became friends, that first winter. I remember the first night I met his father. Robert and I sat on his front porch and his father came out of the house, took a look at my ice skates and asked how far I could skate.

Robert leaped to his feet and said, "Theo Kabel meet my father Judge U. S. Grant." I stood and shook his hand.

"From Dayton to Tadmor." I replied. "Glad to meet you, sir."

The Judge was amazed I could skate that distance. "Robert gets winded skating once around Island Park," he laughed. Slapped a hard blow to Robert's back. "I'll pay you to take him out for some physical conditioning." Robert blushed.

"No need to pay, I'd be glad to skate with Robert." Unknown to the Judge, Robert and I skated to Peach Tree Bend, jumped a passing train and rode back to Dayton many times. Robert feared his father would not permit it and he kept the fact hidden. For the long distance of our skate, Robert stole his father's Cuban cigar and the double-edged guillotine. I smoked and Robert skated.

One day, after our secret trip, I had my fill of Robert and his saying, "The Judge this and the Judge that." I slapped him across the face harder than I meant to hit him. "Shut up, Robert. Stop calling him Judge. Call him father or papa." Whether it was the sting of my hand or the shame, Robert lowered his head and mumbled.

"He makes me call him Judge. And the only time I was brave enough to call him Papa, I was five years old and I tried it out. 'Papa,' I said. I came to at the bottom of stairs with a bloody lip." Robert's glove wiped his mouth and he saw the blood I laid open on him.

"I'm sorry, Robert." I grabbed a glove full of snow and packed it on his swelling mouth. I felt awful. I had not hit anyone since I left the Asylum. I learned the walls of Robert's childhood were papered with schoolmates' taunts due to his father's position for rules. Desperately, I vowed to cocoon Robert from any more of his father's perniciousness. "Come on, Robert, let's smoke."

"I can't! The Judge will smell smoke on me."

"He can't discern his smoke smell from your smoke." I smoked for years. In fact I cut my first cigar tip with my baby teeth. I was five and I lit up in the hen house on Summit Street. A cigar guillotine was foreign to me. No bon vivant in an orphanage. I set about teaching Robert how to warm the ash tip by rotating the cigar end between his thumb and forefinger, how to hold the flame evenly up to the dark brown torpedo and puff lightly. He showed me how to use a guillotine.

I awoke thinking about my good friend. I reminded myself that was then and this is now. I thought maybe the silk threads of the cocoon were not wound as tightly as I hoped. I guess it was easy to tell myself his Highass probably forbid Robert to come to the courtroom. Maybe Robert had enlisted for the coming war. If so, I hoped he knew better than to light three on a match in a foxhole. I yawned. The selection and swearing in of the jury were over.

Concluding witness testimony, my Public Defender asked, "Permission to approach the bench, your Honor."

"Permission granted." The Prosecutor, caught off guard, scrambled to the bench to hear the exchange.

"Your Honor, it will take two days for presentation of evidence."

The Prosecutor's face bloomed in contempt of the Defense's request. His Highass, set to deny the request, noted the Prosecutor's reaction and thought how dare the man try to sway my court in his direction, so he crushed the Prosecutor's unspoken wishes and flinging his supreme authority in the man's face. "Permission granted," he smiled.

The spectator's contempt rained hats and gloves on the main floor, as was the practice.

CHAPTER 12: KABEL DEFENSE

"Extra! Extra! Read all about Kabel Defense of Insanity." William Makely hawked his papers on Ten Cent Row. William had just turned nine years of age, and he was rooted on the sidewalk curbed along the west side of Main Street between Fourth and Fifth Streets. The wiry scrapper had the 'want to' in every fiber of his being. Beneath his cap, his large blue eyes looked out on his challenge of the sales. He was a 'newsy' down through his knickers and into his calf-length, plaid socks. William was fastidious about his appearance. He washed his button down shirt daily. He made sure his suspenders were straight and kept his face, hands and fingernails immaculate. He exuded the confidence of a seasoned salesman, and thought of himself as one, unlike the other rough-and-tumble newsy boys.

William bought his pavement sales spot hemorrhaging noses and handing out silver-dollar-size shiners to any and all would-be usurpers. William though slight in build possessed arms with bottled lightning speed. He could flatten a nose before a usurper could finish asking if he minded that he sell papers at the other end of William's block. William let it be known he owned both corners and the strip between. William held the deed to the best location in town and there he remained, learning about the business world. There he studied people.

William's speed kept him in good stead. He applied it to making a customer's change. Early hour, hurried, businessmen on their way in McCrory's wanted a morning paper, a side to their bacon and eggs. They ate and read at the serpentine counter, the longest counter in America. The counter folded back on itself like the lazing Mississippi River. And 'speed' was the name of the game William played with businessmen. William kept his left front pocket packed with more dimes than an N.C.R. cash register drawer. When the men tossed quarters, William snatched the coins out of the air as flawlessly as Cincinnati Reds catcher 'Hap' Huhn caught Fred Toney. Then William handed over the paper with a dime tucked under his thumb. "Keep it, kid." William thumbed the dime into the palm of his hand and made a half bow.

"Thank you, Sir."

"Yeah, well remember when you make it to the Big Leagues."

"Yes, Sir." He thanked them and scored the running amount of tips, silently in his head.

Second sales wave was women who came downtown to garner McCrory's housewares and ten-cent romance novels. These women sharpened William's memory skills. He took his time and courted them by slowly counting their change and then complimenting them. "Beautiful baby, lovely hat, very pretty gloves." The difficulty lies in remembering what he had complimented on their previous exchange. A woman said, "You said that last week," feeling a repeated flatter was disingenuous. And they severed a tip. So if William was in doubt, he said, "I meant your gloves are so white. Are they new?" Then the woman demurred. "Well, you certainly do keep a white wash."

Sometimes it worked and a tip was brought back. William handed over the change to these women because they felt the need to control the money their husbands allotted. So he indulged them the power they felt when they decided on the amount of the tip and rewarded William.

The last wave of his paper sales came with working women on errands for their bosses. They came to McCrory's to make a quick purchase of face powder, perfume and nail polish. Resting their high-heeled shoes on the rung of the stools they sipped Bubble-Up or Cherry Cokes. William wasted no time on these non-tippers. He was handed the exact price of the paper and he handed over the paper. No chit-chat. No tip.

William's torment for owning the best real estate came with the opening of McCrory's doors. That persecution rode out on the air currents bedeviling him with aromas of hot caramel corn, spice-candied apples and whirling cotton candy. His stomach growled a protest of the day-long apple he nibbled. William gave his widowed mother all of his income. She had seven siblings to feed.

Favorable conditions burned in the noon-day sun when Harry Brightenstein approached William. Harry worked a few doors south of McCrory's and after a late night, Harry came to work in his previous evening wear. No one knew why but figured Harry had left some maiden's bed lacking the time to return home and change into his work clothes. No one asked. Harry kept his 'Never Be Tardy' attendance record come hell or high water and showed up in a top hat and a cane with his usual black pants.

"Are you sober?" His boss sniffed Harry's breath. Harry was. So the boss handed him a monocle and sent Harry back out on the street. Mr. Planters became a walking, talking advertisement and gave away samples of hot roasted peanuts. The people loved the strolling peanut man and sales soared. Harry was happy to get out of the hot shop. He became a very good ambassador. And Harry enjoyed feeding Mrs. Makely's eldest son, William.

Harry fed William throughout the day. "Have some nuts, William," he called out. Then whispered as he poured the peanuts into William's outstretched hand. "They aren't the freshest, but then ye ain't a paying customer. Now are ye?"

CHAPTER 13: DECEMBER VERDICT

"Run, Lola, run!" I woke up drenched in the shallow trench of my cell cot. Nightly, I sweated out the recurring dream where I stood in the welcome cool of August's morning and dawn lingered at the horizon delaying the heat of the day for a few more breaths. I lit another cigarette and a nearby rooster crowed. Crisp, leek-green katydids chirped from hideaways. I watched Mrs. Collin's boarders bang their leave-taking on the wooden screen door. When the Wayne Avenue house cleared, I ground out my cigarette and crossed the street.

I let myself in and passed by the parlor following the din of Lola scraping breakfast plates in the kitchen. Lola was bent down pouring leftover cream in Jasper's saucer. Jasper was pumpkin color and round as a pumpkin, round in his build. He politely meowed appreciation for the calories he did not need nor was he given by our landlady, Mrs. Collins. I watched Lola stroke Jasper the length of his fat self, from the tip of his nose to the end of his tail. Reaching his tail, she gave him a tug that lifted his back feet in the air for a second that he truly loved. Maybe it straightened the kinks in his spine.

"Good morning, Lola." I stood at a distance and kept the table between us. She straightened.

"You should not be in here."

"I know, but I wanted to tell you I registered for the draft yesterday. I can send you money so we can continue to rent here and you will not have to move back to your parents on Newcom Place. After Boot Camp at Fort Knox, we can live together." I laid my draft card on the table and pushed it to her then lit another cigarette. Lola turned her back on the card and moved to the sink. She stared out the window. Time ticked loudly on the kitchen clock. Jasper finished his cream and rubbed up against Lola's beautiful bare legs. The top of his tail moved her housecoat in a fluttering hemline. I ached for her.

"No, Theo. You will ship off to war. The entire country says we are entering soon, very soon. I will not be left alone in a strange apartment on some Army base." She opened the door and let out the cat, then put the last skillet in the soak pan, grabbed my draft paper and brushed past me out of the kitchen. Her scent stayed with me. I had given her that perfume.

I snapped into action and followed her down the back hall and up the stairs to our room. Lola lay on the bed and I took up our room's only chair. "I have a physical examination this afternoon, Lola. I need you to come with me. Please. It is at two o'clock today. I even had enough money for us to take the traction."

"No!" she shrieked.

"Alright, alright." I wanted to quiet her. After last night I was afraid people would hear us and come running, and I think she thought as much because she kept it up. "No! No! No!"

I moved back in the chair. Lola became a different person after our son died. The sparkle of her eyes was gone and she was unkempt. She never gave a thought to fixing her hair, which was something she had always done before Theophilus Junior's death. When she calmed I reached for her hand and she pulled away, rolled over wrapping herself in the chenille bedspread. The open window blew the curtains into the room making the sheer panels spread over her like angel wings.

Lola and I moved out of her parent's house the day following Theophilus Junior's burial, abandoning the walls of our baby's death. I rented this room from Mrs. Collins. Only a few blocks from Lola's parents, she walked there daily. I could not understand why she returned to the place she said she wanted to get away from, but she said they visited on the porch. She never went inside. The move to Mrs. Collins was the first time Lola lived away from her parents. She earned petty cash doing household chores for Mrs. Collins, and it was the first time she had money of her own. I let her spend it freely.

Face down, rolled in the bedspread, Lola accused. "The paper says you are married."

"I know." Dampness beaded my upper lip. "It will give us extra money, Lola."

She rolled back out of the bedspread and smiled softly. "Stupid man! What makes you think if you show them they would be satisfied?"

Sweat dripped from my brow. It was a cruel remark and I was getting very nervous.

"Theophilus Kabel you lied on a government document, a legal paper. You don't need me, just show them a marriage license." She threw her hands to her mouth in mock horror. "Oh that's right. You can't. We aren't married. You made a false statement on a government document and that is a felony. Goodbye. They will put you in jail and there you will rot."

I was physically weak. "We can marry today. Lola, please. I love you. We can have more children." I got out of my chair and her eyes changed color. Cruelty brought a different hue to her eyes. She laughed coldly. Lola was smarter than me in many things, and I didn't know if she was right about the paper.

"You are a stupid man, very stupid. You are an idiot. To marry we would have to wait for blood tests." Then the cruelest words foamed from her mouth in spittle. "You never gave me anything to grow a child since Theophilus Junior died. What makes you think you can perform now?"

Tears blinded me. Lola and I lived under her parent's roof while I struggled to prove my worth to her father's satisfaction. He let me in the door and I worked twelve-hour days at the livery to demonstrate to him I could 'get things right'. Those were his words. I paid her parent's rent and bought their groceries. He kept demanding a bank deposit to show him I could save money. But I never had extra money to open an account. Nothing remained of my paycheck after his bills.

I heard the floor creak behind me, and Lola looked over my head and sneered. The room went black and I woke up on the floor. My chair was turned over and Mrs. Collins stood over me with a board. I braced myself on the side of the bed and got up on my feet just as Lola pulled a knife from under her pillow. She looked at me as if she were behind inches of pond ice, her face as hard as a frozen pond. I squeezed her forearm willing her to drop the knife. Mrs. Collins hit me again and I fell forward.

"Run, Lola, run!" Mrs. Collin's shrill voice rang out and I felt her push me off Lola. Then Mrs. Collins slammed the board into the side of my head. Dizzy, I fought her off and made it down the stairs to the front door. A puddle of onlookers circled Lola where she lay on the sidewalk. I clawed frantically to get inside the human circle and then I knelt down. I lifted Lola's head. She opened her eyes and said, "You killed me, Theo. You killed me."

~ ~ ~ ~ ~ ~

Officer Dayhoff took my arm. "Follow me," he said. The ambulance had loaded Lola and he and I followed. "It is just a few blocks, we can walk it." At the corner of Wayne and Wyoming Streets, Dayhoff guided me inside Central Station. "Let me get you some coffee." We went in his office and he threw his hat on the desk and asked, "Cream or sugar?" I shook my head. Detective Hughes opened the door and nodded at Dayhoff. Hughes was a member of Sacred Heart, a co-usher with me. A man I trusted.

"Theophilus," he shook my hand. "They say you did not run." He laid his hand on my shoulder.

"Why would I?" I was stunned. I didn't understand him.

"It was an accident, then?"

"Yes, a horrible accident."

"I'm truly sorry about Lola. Let's get this paperwork done and I'll get you on over to the hospital." He handed me a yellow tablet and said, "Just write how it happened."

My head ached. "Do we have to do this now? Can I see Lola first?"

"It is procedure. Just write it out and I'll see it is hurried along." Sweat burned my eyes and blinded my writing. I finished and Hughes lit a cigarette and handed it to me. "You did the right thing." I smoked and drank coffee. He read. When he finished, he looked at Dayhoff and said, "Book him." And left the room.

~ ~ ~ ~ ~ ~

Deputy Rice escorted me out the back door of the courthouse for the last time and the only time he gave me a cigarette on the three-hundred and thirty-eight steps. "We wore a path in this lot over the last three months, eh?"

I did not answer.

Rice lifted his hat and smoothed back hair that was not mussed. "You and I dropped a lot of words on this stroll. I wish you luck." He placed his hat back on his head and opened the jail door. At my cell, he unchained me and I went in and laid down on my cot. The vultures I left behind in the courthouse chewed on the fate of my bones.

Throughout my trial, I remained silent. It did nothing to help my defense but I had nothing to say. I left all my words on Hughes' tablet. I was empty.

The sound of my stick raking wrought iron fences

on Summit Street startled me. I sat up confused. What the hell is that? Was I dreaming?

"Wake up, Kabel." It was Deputy Rice running his nightstick along my cell bars.

"Look at the gobshite. Can't tell the difference between a nightstick and a day stick." I put on a show for my jail mates. I was paid in laughter. Anyone who could tease a turn-key was admired. I peered at the clock. Two hours. Two hours, I napped between the time Rice returned me and when he came back for me. A lengthy jury debate is more favorable than a short two hours to decide a man's fate. I knew it. Rice knew it and the jailbirds knew it. The laughter died and I walked in silence. Every man in the jail stood respectfully at his cell door. I smiled and winked or nodded at each one. I heard myself telling them, "It is all right."

~ ~ ~ ~ ~ ~

"All rise. The Honorable Judge Grant presiding…"

The foreman stood in the jury box. U. S. Grant scanned the room and admired himself in the reflection of their eyes. Done with that, he cleared his throat, hit the spittoon and asked, "Have you reached a unanimous vote?"

"Yes, Cock-of-the-Walk." I told myself, remembering the nights the Judge arrived at his house, hanging off the Main Street traction. The motorman would shout, "Master Robert." And I went with Robert to the corner to help him steady his 'Highass' off the back of the traction. His 'Highass' bought rounds for the house, released his shirt tail from the constraint of his pants, loosened his tie and drank the day into darkness. Afterwards he hopped a traction, stood on the back platform and pontificated to the citizens, horses, dogs and cats whom he passed along the way. His unkempt self blew in the wind of the train's speed.

"His Honor is going to fall off someday, I am afraid..." The motorman bit off his sentence though he had a lot more to say. Robert smiled and thanked him and palmed him a big tip. "You take good care of him." Then Robert and I walked the wobbly Judge into the house, put him to bed and closed the door on the already snoring judgeship. Routinely, Robert thanked me and apologized, "He has only been like this since Mother died."

Yeah, I thought, and that has been twenty years.

~ ~ ~ ~ ~ ~

"Yes, your Honor." The foreman's words yanked away my dreamscape. The bailiff received the written decision and handed it over to his 'Highass'. The unfolding of the paper verdict fell harsh on my ears. I shifted my weight knowing the news would be no surprise. His 'Highass' took his time to refold the paper. He dangled the suspense and looked at each juror. He studied the floor and he studied the gallery. They didn't mean a damn. They had nothing to do with the folded paper. But to him, they were his audience. They would be his hangers-on, his cronies at the end of the day. Or so he wanted them to think. Yes, they would be the ones who bragged about 'rubbing elbows with the Judge', when in reality he allowed no one to touch him. If he decided, he would shake a hand, he would touch a shoulder, he would rub a back. He gave the bailiff the paper to walk back to the foreman.

Please God, just let it be over, I wanted to wail. Scream at the top of my lungs. I asked nothing of this court except to attend Lola's funeral. It was refused. That throne-sitting, weak son-of-a-bitch wallowed in the misery of his wife's death, twenty years ago. He drank himself into oblivion every night, while he ignored the child his wife gave him, unless he wanted to abuse him.

I can still see the night I sat on my cot smoking and the clicking of a deputy's routine footsteps stopped at my cell door. Stopped footsteps, in a jail, calls attention like a clock that stops ticking. Everyone looks up. I looked up and the deputy moved his lips beyond my hearing. I walked over to him. He whispered, "She is buried at Woodland." The cigarette fell out of my hand and I stubbed it out. He waited for my reaction. I had none. "I pick up extra money working funerals. I worked hers. You don't remember me, but I came to your house the day of your son's funeral, you know, with Father Osterday."

I shook my head. "I'm sorry, I don't remember."

He veered off the subject. "I really miss Father Osterday. Everyone does. You know, he got transferred? The Archbishop moved the bonny priest and left us with an unworthy one. Not that I'm judging God's men, but my mother believed the path to hell was laid down with the bones of men called to do God's duty but did not bend their backs to help mankind. Sorry, I did not mean to blabber my personal thoughts."

"I didn't know Father Osterday had been replaced."

"If Father Osterday had not been reassigned to Celina, he would be here with you every step of the way. My heart knows that."

"I thought Father Osterday did not visit because I was beyond redemption. He was ashamed of me."

"Oh no. That is not true. Let me tell you the new priest does nothing beyond Mass. A germaphobe, he is! He did not come to our house when my Mother died. Wouldn't you think a man of God would fear nothing? Not germ. Not disease. But this one's bones . . . well I've said enough."

My fingers curled around my bars. "Is . . .is . . .s-s-she b-b-buried next to my son?"

The deputy reached out and laid his fingers on

mine. Tears swarmed in my eyes. He swallowed deep. "I'm sorry." His words rattled against his vocal chords. I jerked away from his touch and sank to the floor.

"How in the hell can a mother do that?" He unlocked my cell, lifted me to my feet and walked me to my cot where I grabbed the sheet and ripped it into thin strips. The deputy made the sign of the cross and left me with my anger.

~ ~ ~ ~ ~ ~

"Foreman, read your verdict."

"We the jury find the defendant, Theophilus Kabel, guilty as charged."

"So say you all?" The topknot flopped forward with the thrust of his gavel. He was as proud as an old rooster dismounting a hen. Officer Rice led me out the door for the last time. A worn-out looking horse, whose sulky days were long over, drew the patrol wagon that awaited me. I climbed on the wagon via two back steps hobbled in chains. Rice maintained my balance then delivered a pat on my back.

"Walk on." Rice called to the driver who flicked the reins. We traveled the length of the back jail lot.

"Whoa." The horse flicked his ears, flared his nostrils and stopped. Mrs. Oldt stood on her porch, her arms crossed over her bosom. Her hair piled on top of her head. It was her attempt to add height to her petite four-foot, ten-inch frame. She leaned against the porch filigree railing.

Sheriff Oldt was highly respected for his fulfillment of his duties, but everyone on both sides of the law loved Mrs. Oldt. People who elected a Sheriff failed to realize they also elect the Sheriff's wife to a job for which she did not run nor might not want. A Sheriff's wife must know how to make frugal one-pot meals. She has to account for every cent of her food budget and keep logs of her expenses. Mrs. Oldt and the Sheriff were two of Dayton's finest people; few cities could boast the same.

Sheriff Oldt was a fair man. He treated his staff and his prisoners with the same manners he offered guests in his formal parlor. I liked to rib him. At the time of my incarceration, I was his longest guest and I enjoyed making the new guys nervous. I remember the time Sheriff Oldt was doing the bed check. He stood before my cell and I said loud enough for all to here. "Hey Sheriff, you did not get my vote. I voted for your opponent. But if I had known what tasty sourdough rolls Mrs. Oldt made, you would have got my vote." The disquiet in the jailhouse was as clammy as a hanging man's palms. As the silence lengthened, I knew I bested the Sheriff with our ongoing teasing. I was wrong.

Gun-slinging, gravely voice Sheriff Oldt looked around pretending he didn't know who was talking. Other eyes shrank from the Officer of the Law. He turned back to me, "Kabel, if I had known you liked Mrs. Oldt's sourdough rolls so well, I'd a issued a warrant for you years earlier." Tickled to the bone, Sheriff Oldt's laughter was like the warble of a tiny sparrow. The jailhouse laughed with him. Thigh slapping followed by whistles turned me away. I laughed at the wall.

Now Mrs. Oldt waved at my departure and I dipped my chin in recognition. I could not wave at the sweet lady and I slid my handcuffs deeper between my knees. As she came down the steps off her porch, I urged the driver to "Move on." The driver feigned deafness. Mrs. Oldt reached the side of the paddy wagon breathless. She smiled up at me and put her hand in her apron pocket then raised a clenched fist. Shyly, I raised my handcuffs.

"Theo," she said uncurling my folded fists of fingers. Her gentleness misted my eyes. She placed a hard object in the cup of my hands, then refolded my fingers for its safe keeping. I whimpered like a dying dove. My brain recognized what my body had forgotten.

Puddin's long ago Christmas note included a gift. I carried the gift in my shoe so I could feel her presence in every place I stepped. "Contraband." Dayhoff called it and took Puddin's gift from me. As I unfolded my fists and looked down at my open palms, swimming in the vision of my tears was Mama's tortoise shell button.

CHAPTER 14: 1917 TRAIN RIDE

The worn-out horse flared his nostril and blew. He rippled his flanks in a job completed and dropped his head in a quiet stop, relieved to be finished with his work. I disembarked under the Union Station clock tower which converted the years of my life into minutes and handed them back to me in memory of when I stood here with Old Graybeard and my brothers. I pushed back hard on the painful memory. Nothing about the train depot had changed. I could see Burkitt's Apothecary sign hanging over the sidewalk up at the corner of Fifth and Wilkinson, and I wondered if he was still alive and then I was glad I didn't know.

A policeman condemned to accompany me on the 10 a.m. exchanged my wrist and ankle cuffs for his own. With the turning of a key, I went from city property to state owned. He moved me up against the waiting train. A Red Cap upon seeing my chains turned his head offering me the privacy of the moment for my escort to get me and my ankle chains up the three narrow steps. I could not help but smile thinking of the Red Cap's little metal stool my brothers chose to leap over.

I took the same fourth seat on the left, next to the window. This time I need not ride backward. When my hand reached for my candy-stuffed pockets my bracelet partner yanked my arm up to the armrest. I smirked. "I forgot. Pockets are forbidden." Then I licked the memory of red licorice whips lingering on my lips.

The train released a cloud of steam and two short whistles. We rolled out of Union Station. I watched landmarks tap dance past my window, a vaudeville routine of Requarth Lumber Yard, Barney-Smith Car Works and Lowell Brother's Paint store. My favorite smell of White's bakery smashed into me. Beyond the buildings, we traveled the length of a large railroad yard strewn with abandon tenders that carried water or oil, cabooses that carried campaigners on back platforms, cattle cars, dining cars and sleepers, hoppers that unloaded through the floors and Pullmans with fancy parlors. The forlorn piece of train stood hooked in pairs and threesomes or in the loneliness of themselves. Doors stood open, maybe by a sleeping hobo getting fresh air. Window shades shown rolled up, rolled down, or halfway in between, like hose on a woman's leg is rolled to the desire of the wearer. Messy, the yard looked like toys a lad abandoned for his Mama's dinner call.

At the end of the yard, the track was divided into a north-bound journey along the Great Miami River where picnickers rode to Indian Lake. Honeymooners took the line to Indian Lake where they could dance the night away in the Pavilion at Russells Point in the arms of their love. Vacationers took entire families and grandparents up to the lake for a respite.

The train I rode headed due east, slowing down for the gentle grade into the narrow gorge that squeezed against the Mad River as it flowed into the city. Then we shot across Huffman Prairie and slithered around the curved, canyon wall past an emerald mural of spongy moss. A long, loud whistle warned oncoming carriages and carts we were coming. Old Graybeard used to tell us about the rattlesnakes in Huffman Prairie that grew longer than most men. He said when they were working to clear the grassland to build the dam, bars gave free lunches to those who brought in the day's longest catch. He said extracted fangs hung like clothesline pins over the bar counter with name of the man who held the record of the day. Fields of grazing cattle and nibbling sheep passed my window at forty-eight miles an hour on the straight run to Springfield.

My escort opened his eyes, looked out the window and with a frown asked, "Did you ever stop to think, train passengers view only backyards? Carriages and cars travel roads past flower-packed front yards, giving the false impression of people's lives. Rail riders see the truth. People's trash, stain hung laundry, shoeless children running amok with dirty faces and snot noses, along with smelly, fly-studded outhouses. Look, right now. There sits a man, pants around his ankles and the door is open on his shitter."

"Guess he don't want to be alone in his own stink." I closed my eyes on the officer but it did not shut him up. I knew all about backyards, more than he would ever know.

"Reminds me of my first prisoner. I was on this route and the Con asked to go piss. I uncuffed his leg chains, right decent of me, I thought, and walked him to the crapper. I told him not to lock the door. I stood outside and waited bracing myself against the rocking of the train. Along comes this ticket taker, looks at me and says, 'He's gone!' I yanked on the locked door. The agent pulls out his key, unlocks the door and the lashing wind hits my face. Brakes shrill the train to a stop, passengers stare up and down the aisle. I run to the back platform and jumped. We were just south of National Road near Xenia-Urbana Pike. There lay the senseless convict pressing a kiss into the soft mud of the Mad River bank. I turned him over and he was still breathing. An ambulance completed his trip. He worked up in the Big House daffy, so daft he won't know when his time is half up."

"I won't know when my time is half up."

The officer opened his mouth, snapped it shut and yanked the cuffs toward him in a show he was in control of my uncaring arm. The arrogant son-of-a-whore kept on talking. "Oh, I get it. It's a joke. On me, right? Joke's on me. You being a Lifer." His breath was worse than my sentence.

We stopped in Xenia, my former home. A Red Cap stepped off the train, placed a metal footstool on the ground, straightened himself and offered his hand to a departing lady. Greeters excitedly waved their handkerchiefs and hats. Others bid sad farewells. I looked for an Irish ginger-haired little boy in the crowd, while the Cock-of-the-Court's words crowed in my head, "Theophilus Kabel, you cannot be reabsorbed into society. Life!"

Vendors strolled the platform. Little boys lugged shoeshine boxes. I looked for Mr. and Mrs. Buckles, maybe holding tickets. I looked for children with ice skates slung over their shoulders on their way to Duck-Butt-Pond. I looked for memories. A vendor, who looked to be made of gristle and bone, trampled over my garden of fond memories and stopped at my window. His mangy hair hung long in his eyes, and he wore a squared box which tilted off his mound of stomach flesh. Leather shoulder straps tethered a box of brown paper wrapped sandwiches. He gave me a lopsided grin of false familiarity and held up a sandwich.

"No." I shook my head at the peckerwood.

"Egg salad." He pressed.

I declined again. His dirt-encrusted fingernails opened the paper exposing pale yellowish white ingredients that he squeezed forward in the bread, as if it would plump up the scanty contents. A liquid of watery mustard oozed over his hand and ran down his arm. Plop, it fell from his elbow and splattered the mess like bird droppings on the top of his shoe.

"Shyster," I screamed on the glass between us. Misled travelers lined his greasy pockets with coins given for watery half-filled sandwiches that they only discovered after the train pulled away from the depot. I wanted to beat the peckerwood into a bloody pulp, the way I beat that Asylum kid, I forget his name, when he called my mother a slut. I hated the vendor. I hated him, his egg salad and his freedom. "May your mother piss on your grave." I flattened my face smoothly across the glass, scumming the window with my spittle. Then I battered my cuffed hands against the glass, my chained mate's included. The cowardly peckerwood jumped back and bled piss down the front of his pant legs. I laughed.

"What the hell?" Yelled my seatmate. "You just pulled my shoulder out of socket." Flushed and angry, he yawed the handcuffs back to the armrest. The piss-legged vendor ran off scattering sandwiches from his box. Two skinny newsboys picked up the wrapped breads and stuffed their pockets, cheating the coward of his money. One boy's head was topped in Irish ginger curls.

"Cowards die many times before their death, but I shall die but once." I closed my eyes on the train's two short blasts.

"Julius Caesar. That is just great. I am a bodyguard to God's Angry Man who can recite Shakespeare to me."

CHAPTER 15: OHIO STATE PENITENTIARY

"Columbus." The conductor stood in the aisle backed against my seat serving as a human shield overseeing the flow of exiting passengers who burned stares in the back of my head. The car resounded with smacks of children's pointed fingers at my chains and stripes.

"Don't stare," people said staring. Parent's threatened, "The bad man will cut your fingers off if you don't stop pointing. That is the boogie man who hides under your bed when you don't go to bed on time." The car emptied of whispers and the conductor stepped away as I hobbled down the three steps into the waiting hands of two armed Ohio State Penitentiary guards.

"Shakespeare is all yours, boys. I've got to be back for Christmas." My chaperone uncuffed himself. A pug-faced, snubbed nose guard with matching jowls cuffed me with new chains and helped me up on the back ledge of an open air Model T Ford, braced up by a one-ton chassis and blazoned on both sides in large white letters, POLICE WAGON, breaking the law that all of Mr. Ford's vehicles wear only the color of black. Two wooden benches stretched along each side of the truck bed leaving a narrow tongue aisle down the center. Four metal ribbed arches held rolled side-tarpaulins on the apex of the arch.

"Watch your head," warned the guard. "Take any seat you'd like. Price is all the same." The gelatin of his jowls shook with humor.

I walked to the front of the truck bed and sat on the end of the bench immediately behind the driver's seat, hoping the largest guard was the driver. Because I was jailed in August, my personal possessions lacked a coat. The penitentiary guards wore heavy military jackets, gloves and stocking caps. They stood beside the paddy wagon making jokes while I shivered, hating myself for looking like a frightened child. We awaited the arrival of other prisoners coming in from other counties. I cursed my trembling. One of the guards offered me a cigarette, "Here is a Christmas present. Don't get ashes on the floor of my truck." I thanked him.

"Where is all this traffic going?" The cigarette giver scanned High Street.

"Mass. People are going to midnight Mass." The two guards jumped. They had forgotten they weren't alone.

"Oh yeah," fat jowls answered.

We three turned our heads and listened hard. There it was again. O Holy Night, the notes fell on me as the gentle down falling snow and I twisted my body. Carolers! Two very round men sausage stuffed in thick, black greatcoats stood in the buttery lamplight of a tall gas lamppost. Bushy muttonchops descended from their black bowlers supporting their fat cheeks. The men held sheet music with their black kid soft gloves for two women dressed in Christmas green coats and who buried their hands in muffs of snow-white rabbit fur. My rib cage contracted. A spasm of croup coughing turned Pug Face around. When he saw I was not puking in his truck, he shrugged and turned away from me. My body weakened inside. Robert's words came back.

"Homesickness is unpredictable. It waits inside you and then attacks every muscle, every bone and every organ. Your lungs lurch for air and your bones ache. Your blood runs cold and your stomach hurls the contents and releases your bowels." I fought to regain my breath. The women's muffs were identical to Mama's.

In the diary of my mind, I could see her in the sickbed. I was playing in her closet and I brought a pretty white muff to her side and asked her why I

126

never saw her wear it. Mama nuzzled the soft fur on her face. "I want it to last forever, Theo." She pulled herself up further on her pillows. Her blood thin-veined hands pushed deeper into the muff. "This muff is the last thing I purchased with my own wages." Her words were dampened with tears. Mama was a seamstress before she married Graybeard. When they wed, he demanded she quit her job while he kept habits and dreams he could not support.

"Oh Mama, you look beautiful." For a moment color splashed across her cheeks and they glimmered a blush. I smiled approval as she posed and giggled. I did not know that was the last time I would hear Mama's laugh.

~ ~ ~ ~ ~ ~

My parents were natives of Tippecanoe, a water town breached by the Miami-Erie Canal and bordered by the Great Miami River. The river ignored the village sliding by soundlessly except for an occasional fish who broke water. The river was uninterested in the village's comings and goings and had business of its own to mind. The canal, on the other hand, collected gossip like flotsam and carried it far and wide. All young people's dating was concentric to the Miami-Erie Canal. In summer heat couples sat in the shade of an overhanging Weeping Willow, holding hands on Lover's Rock. They ate picnics just to the side of the shaded, bridle path and waved to brightly painted canal boats waiting to lock through, Lock Fifteen. In winter, they locked hands and skated over the ice jammed ditch between a string of bonfires dotting the banks.

"I was rushed into wedlock before I had time to ponder the ramifications." Mama said.

Papa said they must marry the coming Sunday, the only Sunday of the month which the priest came down from Piqua. "It is now or never," he told her when she asked for the rest of the month to think about it. Rumors of a gentleman from Tadmor calling on Mama thrice forced Papa's demand.

Then when the time came that Graybeard declared he could not stand idle while the South excused itself from the Union, Graybeard put another baby on Mama and caught a water ride out of town. At the end of the Big War, Graybeard declared his duty done and caught the next boat up the Mighty Mississippi being seduced at every port.

"Until you gambled the last of your belongings on the wharves of Cincinnati," Mama said.

Papa arrived in Tippecanoe on a Saturday so hot, horses refused to swish their tails. After observing the Day of Prayer, he reported to his prewar distillery job. He was given the same schedule. Five days on, a half day on Saturday, Pay Day. Come the first Saturday quitting time, he reported to Paymaster Henry Van Arsdale, a veteran who left his leg on the battlefield at Chickamauga.

"Sit down, James."

Graybeard paused, took off his neck rag and wiped the sweat from his brow and neck under the watchful eye of Van Arsdale. He had a bad feeling. "Bad storm a coming. Feel it? The birds are flying low and silent. Maybe the storm will take down this heat a peg or two."

Henry Van Arsdale never turned toward the window. Never commented on any storm, making James realize this would not be a quick exit. The uneasiness in the room was felt between both men. "I suppose you know I've been told to let you go, James. You are not keeping up with the work." His words opened a plug and drained all the color from James who stared unbelievingly.

"No. I don't know. Why would I know? I know the job." He hissed anger.

"Knowing and doing ain't the same, James."

James sank down on the chair. He hurried his words off his tongue into a stutter. "I kn-kn-know the job. I'll get b-b-back up to speed. Another week. I'll get my rhythm back." Storm clouds darkened the room.

Van's words gelded the man across his desk, and he felt nothing for doing so. He passed it off, blithely, "It ain't me. It is McAllister. He owns the place. Take my advice and don't cause no trouble." He let his words hang over James son-of-Canal-Keeper. The Inn Keeper is the most influential man in any town because Inn Keeps have ready cash in their pockets.

Van's father lost his son's inheritance long ago when he tied everything up in his crops. Two droughts dried the Great Miami River down to the size of Honey Creek and crops became frazzled brown leaves. Corn was pencil thin. Soybeans shriveled and blew away as dust. Van's father lost the farm, the house and the livestock. They were forced off the land and they moved into Mrs. Sullivan's abandoned chicken coup. Mrs. Van Arsdale seemed to evaporate with each dress size. The fact that Henry was an only child affirmed Mrs. Van Arsdale's ovaries evaporated as well. The woman lost her kitchen and was forced to prepare meals over an open pit and set it on an outside table, the only stick of furniture remaining after the sale, along with her iron bed. Henry slept on the dirt floor or in the yard. Worse, though, was his mother demanding he provide meat for the table. It was a task he grew to hate. Sitting before James, now, his face flooded with hatred. The emotional memory threw the smell of dead pigeons in his nose, and he felt the softness of the dead birds. He saw their expressive dead eyes. And heard the last rush of air leave them. He did not think he would ever get hungry enough to kill again. Maudlin, he sat in the memory. The emasculated man sitting across his desk had not stirred. Van mistakenly took it as a sign of acceptance though James Kabel boiled in fury.

James' tongue became tangled in the cotton of his mouth, and he promised himself not to grovel. He sprang from his chair, knocking it backwards against the wall. He forced his gnarled fingers flat on Van's desk and leaned over. "No Irishman fires a fellow countryman. I dragged your one-legged ass off Chickamauga the 20th of September '63. I toted you back to Chattanooga." James screamed at the top of Van's bowed head. "You black-hearted bastard. If it weren't for me, you would have been in Andersonville."

Van stayed cowed under the arch of James' body. Van kept his right hand on the knob of his desk drawer. A gray field mouse squeaked, shattering the silence. He made a dash for the door jam and flung himself, spread eagle, off the top step.

Straightaway, James tossed the desk aside sending papers kite-like in the air. Pencils fell like Pick-Up-Stix. Henry Van Arsdale sat stone still in naked cowardice. Cobra quick, James wrapped his fingers around Van's neck. His strong thumbs pushed Van's vocal cords back in a place that left Van unable to speak, while his eyes bulged broken veins that shot red lines across the sclera. "If I catch you out from behind your desk, I'll drag your one-legged ass back to Chickamauga and let the Rebs have you."

Shortly afterwards James boarded our belongings on the Marymae, a bright purple canal runner. We moved to Dayton leaving Henry Van Arsdale under the menacing eyes of James Kabel's five brothers. As soon as canal gossip revealed the firing of Tippecanoe's native son, a veteran of the Big War, it did not sit well with the town. And since gossip never dies away, it merely changes like the bed of a river over time, the gossip went like this: "The Widow Van Arsdale." No one had seen her husband for months and she never denied it. Well soon gossip became fact when her husband slipped out of town on a moonless night. Widow, she had become, 'grass widow' that is.

~ ~ ~ ~ ~ ~

Another train, another convict arrived at Columbus station. The truck bed shook me with the large man boarding. He moved up the aisle and stuck out his hand. "Robert Lee-Arsonist-Auglaize County." I did not offer my name or hand. I set the parameters of information before I arrived in Columbus. I renounced everything but sleep. I wanted to be left alone. I was going to the pen to sleep away my life. He took a seat across from me. Other stenciled shirts from other counties boarded the wagon, all facing each other, all avoiding each other's eyes. The pug-faced guard with matching jowls walked to the radiator, bent forward and grabbed the handle and cranked the engine into a start.

"He ain't a farmer. He could never grab an udder and twist like that." A convict observed.

"Yeah and I know he ain't got a wife," someone joked.

The driver let out the clutch and we rolled forward as the cranker leaped on the back ledge. "Keep laughing, girls. I'll be laughing last." We lurched onto High Street and passed under the carolers' lamplight. I glanced over at the quartet. One of the men placed his forefinger to his bowler. "God Bless you." I dipped my chin.

"I wish they'd roll down those piss-ant tarps." A convict whined.

"Oh they will. They fold 'em down on your ride out. Dead Man's Ride." It was Robert Lee who brought on the laughter. Everyone but me. In twenty minutes we came to our destination. Stopped by a massive iron gate of evenly spaced bars, enmeshed on both sides into a impregnable stone wall that dwarfed our truck. The wall held no real color. And it held no real hope. On the right the wall butted against a castle that was without a moat.

"I am Robert Lee. I will be your tour guide today. I will also be your tour guide for the next ten years. So says the Judge. Now the men who built your new home worked under rifle barrels trained on their every move. When they completed this grand piece of architecture, those same rifles prodded the same men inside. The magic of it all made them prisoners to their own handy work." The drivers could not hide their smiles. And the wagon load began to talk among themselves. Some of these farm boys had never seen a street with cars, before today. Let alone this city within a city.

A titmouse of a man with whiskers scurried out of the guardhouse and peered through the gate rungs. Our driver passed him a signal as smooth as catcher Hap Huhn squatting behind the dish at Redland Field flashed to pitcher Fred Toney. The gates opened and the little mouse skittered aside.

"A mouse learning to be a rat." The muscled man with sallow skin and eyes the color of clay sliced his eyes sideways at me. He had an abundance of umber freckles thrown across his face so thick that you could mistake them for evidence of a mud fight. His hair, never comb tamed, and arrogance reeked from him. The orphanage was full of people who lived in the mythology of self, the family they came from and what they were going to do in the world. This man was one of them. "This is my fourth invitation to the Governor's tea party. 'Scape', that's me. They don't call me Scape for nothing. I've escaped every jail that ever tried to hold me except this one so they started sending me here. 'Habitual' that's what the last court said. I'm sure glad they don't call me 'habit'. I have grown to like 'Scape'. And I've grown to like it here. I get homesick out there, so I come back.

132

The wagon load laughed. "Hey, Mr. Silence, what are you thinking, over there? It ain't good to get lost in your own mind. Or do you have a mind left? You thinking about your new wife in here or you thinking about the Hole?" Scape's defiant eyes never left my face. I looked straight ahead. I was going to prison to sleep away my days, like county jail. I could see now the pen was not going to be like Montgomery County. It was the same, all over again. Men talking trash, bragging about their game.

"I'm gonna set up shop and get me some 'go-fers'."

"I'm going to own me some bitches and make me some money."

"Yeah, I can see my harem, now."

Nervously, Robert Lee looked to me and then beside me at the man staring me down. "Hey, Scape, where do they keep the women?" The question caught Scape off guard. I knew Robert Lee was helping me out, by pulling attention away. Asylum, Thomas had this knack.

"You are four years late, Little Man. The women heard you were coming up here with your little self and they all moved to Marysville." Snow-covered laughter floated across the wagon bed. Every man on board jerked when the gate slid across the life we led behind us. It wasn't a loud noise but then wasn't the end of the world supposed to be a whimper? A collective somber breath was inhaled, and trash talk was buried deep under loose tongues. Fear was palpable.

I thought about the May day Graybeard led us through the open gateless fence on Summit Street. Our entrance was not as ostentatious as rolling through the Big House Gates, but just as damning.

The guard on the back handed his rifle off to the titmouse. "He will get it back in case you nuts have any stupid ideas." Scape gestured toward the corner turrets, "Those coops crowning the corners are not ornamental.

They house hawks. Armed hawks who ache for rifle practice. Like you ache for a whore."

An acrid odor clogged my nose. I swallowed back bile burning the lining of my esophagus. One convict twisted and puked over the sideboard. Liquid seeped from the eyes of others and one man drooled his fear. We arrived at the intake building and braked.

I was last off the truck and I took my place at the end of a ten-man chained line. The truck pulled away and a guard turned the line around making me first to lead the baby-step shuffle. I led men who obviously had never marched in formation before today. Their jerkiness forced me into looking like a novice cadet and first time ice skater on Duck-Butt-Pond. "If you go down, Mr. Silent, everybody goes down." Scape threatened and I wasn't even registered at the front desk. The line arrived at the front steps and ended our Saint Vitus Dance.

I managed to climb the steps, shackled but unable to grab the handrail. I called out cadence. Men fell into rhythm and Scape screamed. "This ain't no Boot Camp." I quit. "Last taste of freedom, ladies." Snowflakes landed on Scape's outstretched tongue. Tongues rolled out of every convicts' head with the exception of mine. Scape took notice.

~ ~ ~ ~ ~ ~

We were herded into the bullpen. Aligned with state procedure, shave heads, shower nits, new clothes. Two differences in the Admission between orphanages and the Pen were being asked, "Do you have any tattoos?" And we were ordered to stand on a yellow line and strip. Foreknowledge hesitated some of the men. "Pile your clothes on the painted X in front of you."

"Think of the Union Jack, mate." Scape laughed cruelly, and sarcastically added. "Oh, did you think you still owned your body?"

"Shut up, Scape," A guard recognized him. "Scape, I'll take you first, bend over."

"No petroleum jelly, ladies." Scape laughed, unblinking he turned his head sideways, looked down the line and gave me the pig-eye the length of the time the guard performed a cavity search. Procedure over, he stood and asked, "Mr. Silent, would you like to play ball with me?"

"Shut up, Scape. No talking." The guard hit him on the back of his head, but it was a soft hit.

We were searched and released to inmates who gave prison haircuts, and then we were photographed by inmate photographers. Inmates fingerprinted us. The inmate that showered our nakedness had the ability to regulate the nozzle. He used a soothing, pulsating massage and then twisted one-thousand needle pricks that would make a polar bear shiver. Some convicts jumped around, but I figured they just made a bigger target. I stood still, as still as Scape. We all cupped our hands over the family jewels with the exception of Scape. He clasped his hands behind his head and adopted a bored expression as he took the hose nozzle full throttle.

I moved to a counter where a rubber stamp hit a page titled, Prisoner's Registration Book. Time was not wasted to dip a fine quilled pen into an ink well and cursive my name. But I was honored to be recorded on the page's first line. And I said so.

"Do not speak unless spoken to." The duty clerk ordered.

"I know, 'Little Ones are to be seen and not heard.'"

Crack! Thunder boomed in my ears. A black-jack hit my temple and I stumbled. Just as I caught myself on the counter, Robert Lee moved forward and steadied me. "Poor Robert Lee, you get second line." Another blow, that I never heard, dropped me to my knees. Robert Lee leaned down.

"You want to be shot?"

"No, Sir."

"Never touch a fallen convict, unless you want to be shot."

Robert Lee stiffened. Guards pulled me up on my rubbery legs. I laughed at the silliness of the rubber bands I stood on.

"Four-six-one-nine-three, if you don't adapt you will be in the hole before the night is over."

My thoughts sieved through my brain and I smiled from Christmas Past. I was sitting roasting chestnuts on Mrs. Brush's three-legged stool. I licked the memory of egg nog from the lip of my little tin cup.

"Four-six-one-nine-three." He called me back to reality. "Remember your number and do not ever wear another man's shirt."

"Yeah, Sir," I saluted. Feeling lightheaded, I moved with the men into the main hall. We closed in shoulder to shoulder creating a false safety for ourselves and walked the gauntlet.

"Fresh meat," began the insults on both sides of the cell-lined hall. Convicts grabbed through the bars and smeared our manhood, mamas and sisters. They pointed like the brats on my train baiting us. "Hey babe, you want smokes?" The indignities engulfed us.

"Focus on the end of the hall." Robert Lee shored me up. I could feel him trembling on the scariest walk of my life, and I wished James Junior had kept his promise and thrown me off the train trestle.

"Hey, Robert Lee," an inmate called. Robert Lee kept his eyes straight ahead and did not acknowledge his name. We took a few steps and he said, "I guess every once in a while a man gets lucky and guesses an incoming's name." If Robert Lee was hiding a return trip, it was all right with me.

"Four-six-one-nine-three, you are going to help me pee!" The other convicts applauded the poet.

"When you cry tonight, you will call for me." Convicts threw promises at us like children throw blocks. "I'd like to marry that one."

I just wanted it to end.

"I'm gonna make you my wife. That's right. Come on back at dark."

"Put him in my cell, Mr. Guard."

Our gauntlet was followed by the guards, the screw making just as many cat calls and wolf whistles as the convicts.

"You belong to me, remember!" A screw yelled at our heels.

"It's Big Time in the Big House, ladies." Another screw whispered his breath at my back.

At the end of the hall was a door. Like at the Asylum, I stopped. "ORIENTATION," I said and walked in. I took a seat front row center. Robert Lee sat next to me. And though I didn't want him or any friendship, I liked that he was near. The door slammed and all heads turned to the entrant. Except Scape who casually crossed his legs.

The man before us wore a badge that read, 'Donner'. He cracked his billy club on the desk corner splintering wood that bounced off Robert Lee and me. Robert brushed his off. I did not. Donner laid his hat on the desk. He removed his jacket and hung it on the back of his chair. His waist was six linear feet from his spit-shined, high laced, serious stomping military boots. His funnel-shaped body rose out of a thirty-inch waist and widened out into I-beam shoulders. The man's biceps strained against his short-sleeved shirt. His neck flesh threatened to rip the stitches out of his collar. Fork tongue lightning bounced off his bald head into our squinting eyes. Scape whispered loudly, "Donner can press two-hundred and fifty pounds." And Donner smiled at the compliment.

"You ladies do what you are told, everything will be fine." His words were soft as a kitten's purr, but he left you with a feeling he was going to make you his scratching post. The room felt it and remained quiet as a new grave. No heads turned. No eyes met his. He arched his eyebrows. His face filled with rage. "You ladies mess up and you get the hole. If you have designs on being a hard case, drop the thought." Just as quickly as his rage came, it left. He smiled. "Choice is yours."

He lifted a paper from his desk the way an actor holds a prop, "Federal Prison Rules." He gave a recitation that needed no script. Tossing the paper back on his desk, the coldness of his words followed. "This is my house. I run it. I rule it. The only thing you have to remember is do not make me look bad in my house."

Before me stood a man who had not the need for humanness.

CHAPTER 16: PRISON LIFE

Orientation week, a week of lectures and threats, threats and lectures divided our wagon load of convicts from the General Prison Population. It would be the last time we would be with so few people and a time to learn silence is your best friend. And that was a hard lesson for a population that had everything taken away but their voice. Second week, we were rolled out into 'The Yard' like dice. Scape excepted. No one had seen him.

Prison life has a caste system drawn by county lines. County lines encircle feelings of trust. Men from the same county watch each other's back. County pride is a released man carrying a message to a convict's family, a message that would be 'chained inside' by prison censors. I had no interest in counties. I had no outgoing messages.

We were assigned jobs. Captain Faust, assignment officer, summoned us to his office and asked, "Work experience?"

"I was raised on a farm and I am a blacksmith." Faust's assistant threw his nightstick into my ribs. He knocked the wind out of me and knocked me into a chair.

"Address the Captain and use Sir. Stand up like a man."

I grunted. "I am a blacksmith, Captain, Sir."

"Can you handle horses and mules?"

"Yes, Captain, Sir."

"You want an outside job? In a livery or a barn?"

"Yes, Captain, Sir."

Captain Faust looked at his secretary. "Kitchen Duty." The assistant wrote 4, 6, 1, 9, 3 in the column for kitchen help.

"Everyone wants to work outside! You probably

don't know one end from an ass than another. Get out of my office. Go send in the next guy. He will probably say he is a Yacht Admiral."

~ ~ ~ ~ ~ ~

Raymond Jones, self-made Kitchen Warden, ran duty without a broom straw of kindness. His word was law and he didn't get grief. Jones' kitchen had two kinds of food. One was Institution Food, the other Guard Food. The screws gave Jones a wide berth because he took care of problems reducing the guard's load and because he gave them fine dining, not slop.

Raymond Jones was a former Army General's private chef until he sharpened one of his kitchen knives on a man at a poker table. Anyway, Jones brewed coffee for the guards who claimed it to be brewed by gods. And every cream and sugar drinker converted to a no-condiment drinker after swallowing Jones' steaming liquid. Raymond Jones could fold lard into a pie crust and make a flakier pie than your grandmother's. I saw a convict give up his deck of pornographic cards for one cup of Jones' slice of pie.

Raymond Jones gave me no trouble. I left my feelings on the Wayne Avenue sidewalk and I kept numb. I lowered my head and my mouth was locked down. Unlike the others in here, I never wanted to be cream and rise to the top. Crazy men clawed at air giving Jones aerated compliments thinking it would boost them top side. It meant nothing to him, but it hurried the man to a coal-carrying job that left him dirty and outside. And I never saw what Jones had mixed into their meals, but I did see a server slip something from his pocket and cover the man's tray with dark gravy.

~ ~ ~ ~ ~ ~

My prison days were ended by washing up and going back to my cell where I waited to march to mess hall with my block, Cell Block G. I ate second shift of the double shift in the overcrowded prison. Supper finished, we filed lock step back home to our cells. Eight o'clock Firestone Theater was my treat to myself. I was lucky enough to have a radio.

On this particular night, Jimmy Henderson-Montgomery County-Armed Robbery jumped in line behind me. Jimmy's crime was being handed an empty gun. He stood face to face with a witness he couldn't kill while his partner ran away. Well that is his story. Jimmy had a need to prove something but never with me. He lacked something in his life and it might have been friends. County lines build strange friendships. I stayed on the quiet side of him, and I observed years of no one being able to tell him anything. He was always on the muscle, and he lived most of the last five years in the hole. It changed him. His mind stopped working on all pistons, if it had ever run fully. I should have seen it coming but Jimmy played Whist and I liked to play. He would brag we were 'counties', and I stayed too long on the safe side of humoring him.

Our bets never had problems but as Jimmy changed over the years a meanness grew in him. Our last bet was on the Chevalier vs. Carnera fight. I took Leon Chevalier and he took Carnera, the Ambling Alpine, who had been a circus entertainer in Italy. When Carnera disembarked in Philadelphia, his size attracted boxing promoters. He stepped out from under the Big Top and into the boxing ring.

Jimmy had slipped into line behind me on our way out of mess hall. "Pay up, you gobshite." I wanted him to know I knew he was back there.

"Go to hell."

After more steps on the queue, I said. "Jimmy, the referee raised Carnera's hand. Sixth round. Both men standing." Jimmy could not read. So, I read him the comics and the Sport's page. I read him the article headlined, *'Bob Perry, Chevalier's Second, Threw In The Towel'*. "You know, Jimmy, Bob Perry surrendered Chevalier's fight."

Jimmy's foul breath curdled my blood. "Referee, Toby Irwin, declared Carnera the winner. That is what the radioman said. That is what I heard. That is what I know. You made up your own words pretending that paper said you won."

"Kiss me bollocks, Jimmy. The fight was phony. New York guineas backed the thrown fight and paid Bob Perry to throw in the towel so Carnera would win."

A screw sprang up beside me and smacked his black-jack against his open palm, then struck the wall beside my head. "Which one of you sissies want to sleep in the hole?" The sound of marching prisoners was his answer. "That is what I thought. You maggots want to be held by your wife tonight. So shut up!" He stopped and watched us march away.

Jimmy and I rounded the corner heading up the west hall and Jimmy leaned forward and growled, "A bet is a bet. You lost. Prick."

"You better back down, Jimmy. My bet was on the first man who ever knocked your man down and he did."

"But he got back up. He was good to fight more rounds."

Guard Gimbaroni rounded the corner and pulled me out of line. I was on my way to the hole and did not give a rat's ass. "If the guinea won, why are they still holding his purse?" I called over my shoulder to Jimmy. The sound of my melon head breaking open was heard the length of the hall. My eyes kaleidoscoped into swirling blackness and I melted on the floor and urinated myself.

"Stepping out, Sir?"

"Step out." Gimbaroni answered. Marching men flowed out and around me the way a river diverts a protruding rock.

I awoke in Major Scott's office. He was pasty white, the color sun never reached. Even his eyes lacked color. His basement office was the gate to hell. It opened the way into the Hole. No one knew if Scott had a wife or a home. He never was absent from his office. Scott sent men to the hole if he thought the guy was smoking in bed. If you got accused of stealing another convict's radio, Scott holed you by the permission of his court. If he thought you smuggled food from the dining room, he questioned you in his court and always found you guilty. All Scott's interrogations delivered a man to the hole.

"Hole him!" If he thought you gave him the pig-eye. "Hole him" if you were accused of spitting on a sidewalk. "Hole him!" If he thought you thought you were a bad ass. His long list of offenses changed with his mood. He was known to have put a man in the hole for life when the convict knocked out Scott's front tooth. Or so they said about his missing tooth. Scott's court found me guilty, and his missing tooth smile was as angry as if I had separated his tooth from his mouth. "Three days in the Hole," he fined me.

I opened my mouth and he cocked his head. "Oh, three is not enough, eh? Hole him a week." I shut my mouth. "This one needs a tune-up." He chopped my shoulder with the blade of his hand and knocked me off my chair. I hit the floor and Scott lifted me up with the toe of his combat boot. The kick was stronger than any I received from a mule.

Two screws lifted me under my arms and dragged me to the hole. My legs were useless. My rib was broken and I forced myself not to cry. When the screws opened the door a funk hit me as hard as smelling salts burn eyes. It was at that time I realized a fact in prison is futile. Blackness of the hole hid the hand I held before my eyes. And it hid the fact, I won the bet.

A pair of footsteps walked away. I waited, huddled against a dank wall listening. My ears tensed in the wait. I curled myself, womb-tight, against the vicious bites of I don't know what. My skin crawled with vermin. I closed my eyes quickly and felt legs crawling on the outside of my eyes. I squeezed my lids, tight against their welcome. Making a choice, I took off my shirt and wrapped my head against lice, mice and centipedes entering my nose and ears. I felt a rat nudge his nose under my shirt wrapping. His nose met mine and I swatted him away. The coldness of the room absorbed my body heat and left me shaking uncontrollably.

"You think years of avoiding the Hole earned you easy time?" The footsteps I was waiting to leave spoke. "Scott hates 'perfect timers'. You lived prison life with perfection and he was waiting for you to break down. He waits for all you perfect times to mess up, and he salivates over holing perfect timers for the first time. He takes a personal affront to any prisoner who thinks he can come and go and avoid the hole. Cause you can't. He brags that everyone comes to his party, and he takes it personally if you wait years to do so. You spent thirteen years avoiding The Scott Hotel and he hates you more than a repeat offender. Now if he gives me the order to 'fine tune you', I will beat you senseless or I will lose my job. I got eight children and a wife counting on Friday's paycheck. The only reason your first beating didn't remove your sanity is because he wants you alert enough to remember his Hotel. Oh, you will be back. The ones who stay out of the hole the longest, come back with the most frequency after the first visit. It just is. The next time Scott will make you cry like a baby for your Mama. The last perfect timer Scott ordered a tune up on was dragged bleeding into the hole. I cannot say if he bled to death in the hole, but

I will say the man never saw the inside the infirmary." The footsteps faded down the hall.

Inhuman howls raged twenty-four hours in the hole. Syllables, spoken in tongue, made me believe the poor soul was already held in God's hand.

~ ~ ~ ~ ~ ~

"You are free." Uncomprehending the meaning, I remained where I was. "You are free, let's go." The door stood open and I crawled toward the light. I reached the hall and curled up like the cinch bug I had become. "Light makes you do that." I could not open my eyes to the voice. My brain was razored by the intensity of the light. I lay dazed at a screw's feet. He allowed me time then pulled me up on my feet and slowly walked me through the Gate of Hell. He took me to a shower and hosed off my body. I cannot tell you if the water was hot or cold. My skin had lost feeling. I received a clean grey uniform and I got my sea legs back. He led me out in the hall of men returning from mess and I fell in with them. I recognized my cell and peeled off the line under the watchful eyes of screws posted at each end of the tier. I was home. It was five o'clock.

Jimmy Henderson-Montgomery County-Armed Robbery entered the cell directly across the tier from mine. He gave me the pig-eye. The screws began the nightly lock down. They hurried because it was the end of their shift, and we liked that because only after a cell was locked could a prisoner talk. I lay down on my bunk, my most prized possession. No bottom bunk sleeper ever had a shank driven into his back. Top bunk men were shanked often and fast. In fact, so fast blood would bubble out of the man's voice as he gave a silent scream. Second prize was my radio. I had the top two comforts of prison and Jimmy had none, but that did not keep him from mouthing a silent threat to me as a guard locked his cell.

"Judas Priest." I sat up. A man in my cell leapt off the top bunk and stood staring at me.

"Tommy Holland-Coshocton County-six-to-thirty-burglary. People call me Holl." He offered his hand.

I turned away ignoring him. Holl jumped back up on his bunk never touching my bed. I smiled. He had been inside before. A prisoner code of conduct was to never put your feet on another man's bunk.

"I got out of Orientation after mess hall closed. I'm hungry. You got any crackers or candy?" A cricket chirped in our cell. "I've got Camels." Holl sweetened the deal.

"Pack?"

"Yep, unopened."

"I just got out of the Hole. I haven't eaten a meal in one-hundred and sixty-eight hours. I pulled a hunger strike but got hungry and slurped that slop and went back on strike. I need my candy bar. Eat that chirping cricket."

Holl laughed. "What? Are you kidding me? If you knew me, you'd know I eat only chocolate-covered crickets. The hole, eh? I thought you looked like hell, figured it was either the hole or the infirmary." Gravity brought me a pack of Camels. "Sorry about the hole," he said. "Keep your candy."

The rustling sound of cellophane hurried my last cigarette before the smoking lamp went out. I was barely able to sit at our cell table, I was so weak. But smoking in bed would have put me back where my morning began. I tossed a candy bar to Holl who sat dangling his legs from his bed. Behind him Jimmy Henderson glowered and it almost made me laugh. There he stood with raccoon circles around his eyes. He gripped his bars trying to look mean, and all I could see was torn skin, busted knuckles and lost teeth. He was a portrait in what happens to a con who is the cause of another man going in the hole. Jimmy would have been jumped before I reached Scott's office. Fast and hard, he would have been beat. The wrath of convicts in the recreation yard will make Jimmy hug the wall for the rest of his prison term. No hoops will he play. No bars will he chin-up on. No one will trade with him or talk to him. Once you hole a man your social life is over. The screws know it and that is why they release a man forced to walk the parameter of the yard.

I stood and went to my window. How long it seemed since I had looked outside. Jimmy felt the cut of our relationship and he hated Holl for replacing him. "Hey, Theo." Jimmy called to my back. "Pitchers Eugene Trace and George Orndorf just got sent to Peoria, Cincinnati Farm Team."

I never turned away from the window. The gobshite begged for my attention. "Giants are off to a bad start. Babe Ruth and Mark Koening are barely hitting their hat size. Let's make a wager. What do you say?"

My back remained facing him.

CHAPTER 17: WARDEN ASHWORTH JACKSON

Warden Ashworth Jackson stepped out on his front porch minutes before the six o'clock changing of his guards' shift. Finished with dinner, he sought solace on his porch. He could smoke and think and take in the fresh evening air. His first job was School Master and he was no taller than his eighth grade boys. He then and there decided if he was to get respect he must dress immaculate, never smile, and stand very erect. Being immaculate in dress was not hard. He was an only child and his mother never allowed him to get dirty or play with other children. He did not laugh with other children, so the only time he smiled was into his mother's face and that was on cue. She was a very stern woman and never smiled except to tuck him in at the end of her weary day. His mother was a tiny woman, and he towered over her making him unaware of his shortness. His teachers were tall and he just thought he would be tall when he was the teacher. Stretching his frame took a concentrated effort. And his back expressed the agony of his enforced stance. He wanted respect and he demanded respect. His wire-rimmed glasses-circled eyes held no mirth for his class. He wanted everyone to know he was in command throughout his rise to the top. His second job was field officer at the Mansfield Reformatory. His promotion to Warden of Ohio State Penitentiary he felt was partly due to a lifetime of making himself a hard vertical line with eyes that could lock down hard on anyone.

Recently, age had deposited a double chin and paunch on the Warden. He detested the softness of age. His eyebrows grew into soft flowering masses of hair he turned to moustache wax to force them into hard-looking, horizontal ropes above his glasses. He wore a tie to every meal and he changed his shirt twice a day. And added the cleaning bill to the prison's budget. Ashworth Jackson never made a needless move. He was not flowery or flowing in his actions or his emotions. Everything about him was under very tight control. And he never used profanity. Oh, not because he was religious but because he felt it was a show of weakness in a person. "One should be in complete command of superior thoughts and a superior vocabulary in dealing with students and in dealing with subordinates."

Warden Jackson spent his leisure hours falcon hunting on his farm he owned in Botkins. If he had not the time to travel to Botkins, he could be seen standing on the banks of the Olentangy hammering a catfish to death. He hated catfish. He hated the smell of them frying in his mother's wrought iron skillet. From April to November his mother fed him catfish. They never had meat after his father had run off. He never asked why they couldn't have meat. And he never asked why his father ran off.

But tonight they celebrated his wife's birthday and his daughter, Vivian, hosted the lavish affair. Vivian ordered a standing rib roast from their Trustee Cook. Raymond Jones requested he do the birthday cake. And it was beautiful. The Warden gave his wife a string of pearls and then excused himself to the front porch. When he closed the door on the party he reached in his vest pocket to retrieve a cigar. "hecho a mano," handmade, he praised the Havana and drew it slowly across his upper lip enjoying the aroma. It was a beautiful night to the close of an Easter weekend. He placed the cigar in his guillotine. Then slammed the hidden razor blade and snapped the tapered end of the cigar all in one stroke.

Vivian stepped out on the porch and came quietly to her father's side. She scratched a match into a light and he drew the flame into his tobacco. Slowly he turned the brown, fragrant weed clockwise obtaining an even light and Vivian blew out the flame. For several long breaths she waited as her father established the light. Then she pushed the ashtray across the rattan table closer to his chair. He shook his head. "Let's walk." She stood back and allowed the flame to release the flavor her father sought, then she placed her hand in the crook of his elbow and he patted her. "Are they talking philosophy?"

"Yes," Vivian gave a silly laugh and he smiled. His daughter had been born with a gift of laughter. It was like a bubbling thing that just arose from her being. She invited Father Bernard, former prison chaplain, to the family celebration tonight. Her mother was very close to Father Michael Bernard.

"Bernard, like the dog. Father Bernard." The priest introduced himself to Mrs. Jackson when she first stepped inside her new life, inside the prison walls. Mrs. Jackson feared everything about the new world her husband had moved them into. She feared Trustees and was against them working her house and tending her gardens. Father Bernard worked a miracle in allaying Mrs. Jackson's fears. From morning to night, she moved easily among the help. She even rode privately to market with a Trustee driver who carried her on errands.

As they strolled along the porch that wrapped around the house, Warden Jackson said, "I remember the Christmas Eve you were born, Vivian. Your dark chestnut hair and large chocolate eyes. You favored your mother's family. Everyone in Botkins remarked on your beauty. Indeed you have grown into a fine-looking woman."

"Thank you, Father." She squeezed his arm. Vivian bobbed her hair in the latest craze with marcel waves over her left eye, and Warden Jackson felt it gave her a softer more approachable look than her mother's severe style. Mrs. Jackson put her hair into a wrapped bun at the nape of her neck the day Vivian was born and kept it so every day after. Vivian tried to coax her mother into a change of hairstyle and Mrs. Jackson simply dismissed the subject. Then this past week, she hit the gist of the matter hot and heavy.

"Please, Mother, just try it for your birthday party. If you try it and don't like it, we can change it back."

"Vivian, I want no more talk about my hair. I cannot change it back if it is all chopped off. And I am Matron of the Penitentiary. The state pays me to do a job. I keep a household budget. I am paid to look matronly."

Warden Jackson paused at the side porch looking over his domain. Vivian slipped her hand away and moved over to the other side of the porch leaving him alone with his thoughts. Ashworth Jackson stewed in the thoughts of his critics. He recalled the family's move to Spring Street vividly. He brought along Mother Hough, his mother-in-law, inside the prison after his wife had night terrors of the move. She would wake up sweating and screaming against her dreams of what the move held for her. Jackson thought it would calm his wife to have her mother move in with them. Then as it turned out, both women huddled in fear of Trustees' eyes. They spent their days in the sewing room and had Vivian bring lunch to them. Mrs. Hough and Mrs. Jackson attended the dining room table, only if the Warden was present. Then Mrs. Hough died. "That was the start of public criticism." Jackson spat out his thought and the Havana lost its flavor. He stubbed it in the ashtray.

He stared up at the stars while his thoughts rattled in his head like the tip of a rattlesnake's tail. He had been respected at the prison until then and respect was all he asked. He struggled to form his loose thoughts. Orville Faraday broke up his earned respect, but what else could I have done, he questioned himself. My wife was prostrate with grief. Her mother was dead and the doctor said, "You must not leave your wife. You must remain at her side. She might not come out of her hysteria."

"I telephoned Governor Whitaker. The Governor would not give Faraday a reprieve. The prisoner has already occupied Death Row for ten years," he told me. "Get Dean to preside over the execution. It is within the law to assign the Chief Deputy. And that is what I did. Chief Deputy Dean Lovely stood in for me."

Warden Jackson took up pacing the front porch boards thinking everyone has an opinion. Everyone is a lawyer, and the public think they know the law. Anger reddened his nose. If they are convinced they know the law, they should lawyer every convict I feed. Half of them don't even attend their kin's trial but they know how the law reigns when that kin becomes a ward of the state.

He sank into a chair and placed his head in his hands and mumbled, "My conversation with the Governor is ruled by confidentiality. Faraday is just as dead as if I attended the execution." He stood and shook his fist at the night. "The public is full of twaddle." Then he knitted his brow and sat back down never noticing the tiny flames, the length of a child's sparkler. The red strings of heat flickered, ducked and peeped all the time scattering blisters across the roof of Section I. They danced frivolously independent of each other until joining into a large tongue that lapped Section H and G rooftops.

Vivian disappeared into the house. A few minutes later she stood at the door and sifted her words through the screen. "Father, someone phoned in a fire call from the prison."

Jackson nodded thinking, two or three times a month convicts, usually 'K' Company, start a fire of toilet paper. And even when he rationed toilet paper they managed to build up a supply to ignite. It was probably the same tonight. The guard would rush the fire with a bucket of water and it would be out before he got there. Guards hated the paperwork they must turn in from a fire, they hated calling the Warden and they hated most a fire at shift change. He knew they took it out of the prisoners' hides in various covert ways. Guards whacked them, shorted their food portions and stole their toilet paper forcing them to wipe with the only sheet they had for the week. But their war was their war, prisoner and guard, and it was silent.

He walked to the door, Vivian returned and handed him his rifle and he stepped off the porch headed to the Deputy's office to sign off on the coming report.

CHAPTER 18: FATHER ALBERT O'BRIEN

"Perdition," Father O'Brien entered the gates of Hell. Twenty minutes earlier he was engaged in a pre-dinner drink and sharing a joke at Aquinas College with fellow priests. The phone rang and Brid Doyle, housekeeper and cook, turned down the fire on the simmering gravy and hobbled down the hall on her painful bunions. She struggled with the mouthpiece on the wooden box hanging on the wall. Her arthritic fingers worked to pull it toward her five-foot-nothing frame. She scolded, "Always leaving the phone pointin' toward heaven. Inconsiderate, that's what it is." Brid never said this to the priests. She held her tongue fearing God might not favor her criticizing His worker bees. Father O'Brien presented her with a stool for Christmas one year, but pride kept her from using it unless the rectory was empty. Brid wrestled the mouthpiece down and her bunions thanked her. On those occasions when she had to stand tip-toed, her bunions and gout punished her.

Brid became a widow when she was young and had no children. She talked to her parish priest about entering the convent. "Maybe that is my calling," she said.

"I think you could better serve the Lord as a cook, here at Aquinas. Our cook returned to the Homeland and we need someone immediately." Father Spencer smiled and took her hands in his. "I've tasted the pies these hands have produced."

"I'll have a look around," she said and went into the kitchen. Brid looked at the clock and began banging pots and pans. Father Spencer went to the swinging kitchen door, put his ear to the wood, smiled and walked away. Brid fixed supper that day and forty years later she still held Kitchen Court without saying she would take the job.

Pulling the fluted black speaker down to her mouth, Brid answered. "Aquinas Rectory, God Bless You."

In the dining room, down the hall, Father McEniry stood at a sideboard that stretched the length of the wall. He set the decanter down and replaced the elegant, silver stopper. The pineapple cuts on the crystal glass bounced beautiful light on the room's walls. "Every good story requires a drink."

"Amen," the priests chorused. The fraternity of priests shouted out phrases from Father McEniry's much-repeated repertoire.

Down the hall, Brid removed her hearing aid from her 'best ear' and pushed the telephone receiver hard against her ear. She stuffed her forefinger in the bad ear and closed out the noise of the joking priests. "Repeat? Once again please." The news was the same. "I will tell him immediately. Thank you." She left the receiver dangling by the cord and leaned against the wall. Her hand on her chest, she took deep cleansing breaths. Tears clouded her eyes. She focused on the dining room's swinging door and threw her shoulder against it. The door swung open harder and wider than she had ever passed through and she stumbled in. The priests' smiles froze on their faces, and Father McEniry caught Brid in his arms. His drink, still in hand, wetted the two of them. Brid was ashen. Carefully, Father McEniry lowered her on his vacant chair. Deacon Stahl dipped his napkin in his Waterford glass and laid it on the back of Brid's neck. "The Penitentiary is on fire, Father O'Brien." He stood. As he came around the table, Brid reached in her apron pocket and palmed off her emerald rosary beads to Father O' Brien. Voiceless, the men filed out behind the Chaplain of the Church-Behind-The-Walls.

Brid looked over the table at the unfinished

dinners. She crossed herself and began to pray for what her religious sons would face. "Godt'e Dia leat." May God go with you, and she laid her head on the table. The front door closed and her head snapped up. She quickly got to her feet. Never in forty years had she sat at their table. It didn't seem right. The burning gravy turned her away from the table.

~ ~ ~ ~ ~ ~

Father O'Brien led his brothers down Spring Street. They reached the prison and came toe-to-toe with Warden Jackson. "Father," he nodded transferring his shotgun to the shoulder away from the priest. "Father," he added. "The guards will let you in."

"Are you on your way in?" Father O'Brien asked.

"No, smoke exacerbates my asthma."

Stunned, Father O'Brien stared. No one moved.

"Doctor's orders," Jackson said weakly. "The guards will let you in." He gestured with his free arm. Father O'Brien walked on thinking if the Warden was outside the fire must not be serious and it was probably more smoke than flames. The guard opened the gate and the priests walked into the inferno.

"Perdition," Father O'Brien said. He and the priests lifted their cassocks and made their way over the maze of engorged water hoses. "Search for the living." His calming voice held command at a time when the felt he had none in a yard already littered with bodies. "Give last Sacraments," he ordered his brothers. Statues in black heretofore moved out among the chaos.

"Father, Father," O'Brien looked up to see a burning man pull frantically on the iron grills of his cell window. He had smashed out the glass and severely cut his hands. "Father, please . . .save me." Father O'Brien could see the firemen's ladders ended half way up to the man. Nervously he rubbed each bead of

Brid's beads between his thumb and forefinger. He looked around and saw guards running and shouting orders. Firemen put their backs into moving around pulsating hoses that alternated between having water and not having water, as onlookers drove over hoses connected to outside fireplugs. City Police stalked the yard. They culled first-tier prisoners into groups away from firemen. And the fire continued eating its way from the roof downwards. National Guards held guns aimed at the courtyard melee.

"Hell has surely broken open." Father O'Brien called on his God. He made the sign of the cross at the burning man in the window. "Look down upon him, good and gentle Jesus." Tangerine flames burned holes in the night sky, and the man in the window flapped white wet, sheeted arms, ethereal-like, his wings billowed and he was already an angel. "Dante's Inferno could not be worse."

Rolling black smoke came down like a shade on the burning man then lifted to reveal nothing. Father O'Brien stared at the empty window knowing the man was already seated in heaven. He turned to step and at his feet lay a man who reached up. Father held his hand while the burnt man died.

"Father O'Brien." Standing at a cell window was a man who joined church at Easter Vigil. The parishioner called out. "Shoot me, please, Father!" The sickened priest called on God not to forsake the man who exploded in flames the color of thick rich Irish whiskey.

At another window flesh of hands wrapped around the steel bars, attached to no man. A deadly balloon of smoke and gas floated through the bars drifting up and away like a child's balloon; it carried the breath of suffocating men. And the forty-two-year-old priest from Tipperary sobbed. "Throw open the Gates of Heaven," he begged, "And deliver these men."

Father O'Brien's lilting brogue and his sparkling blue eyes were known everywhere in the prison. He celebrated Mass, administered sacraments and walked inmates to their execution. He mixed it up on the basketball court and sat quietly with men on death row. His star rose fast in the four short years he served the prison. Inmates, guards, administrators, Protestant and Catholics alike respected the man. He was held in high esteem.

Calvin Harvey-robbery-Lima saw the priest and ran up to him and yanked on his sleeve. Bitterly, he cried out. "Charles burned up!" Charles was his brother and both were lambs in Father O'Brien's fold and served at the altar yesterday. Vividly, Father recalled Mrs. Harvey requesting a meeting last fall. Their mother rushed her words fast and furious.

"Father, the keys were in the car."

"Let's sit down." He pointed to a small table with two hard chairs. Mrs. Harvey sat and began pushing on her knees like she was kneading dough. Her eyes flitted around the room, never landing anywhere.

"Charles borrowed the neighbor's car and took it on a joy ride. I know it was wrong, so does he." She moved her hands from her knees to her purse. "Charles replenished the gasoline and parked the car in their driveway." She hesitated, opened her purse and removed a freshly ironed, white handkerchief. "It was night and the neighbor's were asleep. They did not miss the car." Folding her handkerchief, she replaced it unused, back in her purse. "Someone saw him driving down the street and told the neighbor."

"I read Charles' trial notes. I know he admitted guilt and apologized to the neighbor and promised a year of their yard work for restitution."

"Yes, Father, and he mowed their grass for them for free every Thursday before that," she sobbed. "For thirty years, we got along. On Saturday's Charles washed their car gratuitously. He liked to touch cars, clean and wash them. He even whisk-broomed the inside chairs of the machine."

"Mrs. Harvey, the judge had to go hard on him because it was a night burglary." The priest struggled to make her understand. He reached over and patted her hand and told her the neighbors would have to answer for themselves when they faced their Maker. "You must be strong for your sons."

She fought back on the sentence. "Charles had no previous record. I think they meted Ed's crime on Charles."

Ah, there is the burr. Tis out, she opened her underlying belief. Father shook his head. "Tis my belief judges keep the lines of law straight. They would not punish a lad for his brother's misdeed. Maybe tis a good thing that will scare young Charles away from any further mischievousness." His eyes sparkled. "Charles became an altar server with his brother. I think they are on the right path. I will keep in close contact with him and Ed as well," he soothed Mrs. Harvey lifting her spirits.

~ ~ ~ ~ ~ ~

"Dumb ass kid." Ed stood crying beside the priest, and Father put his arm around him. "Father, he told me he did it to follow me to the Big House." Ed walked away talking to the night air. Father O'Brien pulled a notepad from his pocket and began a list of people he would call personally. Mrs. Harvey was first on the list. Albert O'Brien had the task of informing the mother that her twenty-two-year-old son was dead for returning an undamaged car, with the gas arrow on full. His stomach returned his pre-dinner bourbon and he spewed it behind a bush. He wiped his mouth clean and went into the carnage.

He came upon charred bodies with faces burned beyond recognition. He began administering final Unction and not caring if the corpse was Catholic or not. Father McEniry came up to him and Father O'Brien pointed out the hospital and said, "Check the Wards." He ushered newly arriving clergy to follow Father McEniry and then he moved up to a burning building. As he stood next to the door he heard a radio overhead and he looked up.

"Gangway," Scrape yelled coming out the door. "Hey, Father. You are going upstream." Scape and another con carried a body across a small clearing and dropped their burden on the water-soaked lawn among other bodies. Coughing, their blackened faces almost made them appear headless in the night. Fighting hose lines laid up the flights of stairs, the men of Company K stepped gingerly down the stairs with limp burdens.

Father O'Brien strained to listen above him. He grabbed Scrape on the con's return trip and pointed up. "Yeah, Father, ain't that something? They are broadcasting the fire live into America's living rooms." The priest knees weakened and Scrape supported him.

"How must their parents feel?" Father O'Brien righted himself.

"Yeah, well feelings are checked at the gate, in this place, Father." Scrape returned to his brothers of Company K who were rescuing corpses. Three white medical uniforms tramped between the priest and Scape. And flames spread to the sixth range. Crowds filled the front lawn and automobile traffic jammed the streets. Guards stationed outside dropped their rifles and picked up sub-machine guns and drove back the bystanders.

"Get the hell away from that building." Thunder split the air. A fireman tackled Father O'Brien, threw him over his shoulder and carried him out of harm's way. Bricks crumbled and fell like loose cheese. Bricks and debris hilled the ground where Father O'Brien had just stood. Hot embers were flung out on injured men littering the yard and burying them in thick dust that burned off all the oxygen under the rubble. Moans leaked from under the funeral pyre. Firemen, prisoners, and police dug through the debris burning their own hands in an effort to open air pockets for the men lying under the bricks. Everyone worked feverishly over the mortar. It was an impossible situation.

"Jesus, Joseph and Mary. You are a damn priest." The sooty fireman faced the man he had just tackled, and he set about wildly making an effort to dust off Father's vestment.

"I'm no worse off, my lad."

"Father O'Brien," a young priest softly touched his sleeve and pointed behind him where Mother Superior from St. Rose convent flattened her face against the hard rails of the gate. She held a death grip on the bars. Behind her stood her 'Domincanettes' as the men of Aquinas House teased, out of Mother's earshot. The Dominicans served in the hospitals and they all were waving and shouting at him. He approached the gate and leaned forward, "Mother Anne." A National Guard lowered his rifle and positioned it between the priest and the bars of the gate.

"Harry, remove that terrible thing, now!" Mother Anne's eyes blazed at the soldier. Her voice knocked him back to his elementary school days where he was known as 'Harry'. Mother Anne was Principal of St. Ignatius. Harry placed his weapon at Parade Rest hoping he did not look as wilted as he felt.

Mother Anne leaned into the rungs of the gate and Father O'Brien bent down to her lips. "We are here to aid the dead and dying but are forbidden to enter." She then straightened. Her accusatory eyes burned into Harry, who kept his eyes lifted over her head, afraid to look upon Reverend Mother's face.

"State Official mandate," Harry regained his speech. Nervously, he added, "Risk to the Sisters. Sir," adding a salute. Oh, hell, he thought. It was too late to undo his salute. He snapped the offending hand to his side. "Sorry, Sir . . .Uh, Father, sir. Sorry, Father." Harry's skin deepened in color as his blundering grew.

Repeatedly, he swallowed back his Adam's apple. His capacity to think fled. His eyes searched a guard of higher rank. None could be found. He had two pairs of eyes staring at him.

"All women," his voice quaked and his palms beaded sweat. "Orders, no women may pass." He jerked his rifle off Parade Rest and cradled it in his arms trying to rid himself of the schoolboy-on-display.

"All women?"

"That's right, Father. Mother Superiors, Novices, Postulants, all women."

"Yes, that about covers it." Reaching through the gate, Father O'Brien patted Mother Anne's hand. "Wait near. A call just went out for all medical students in the area. I'm sure they will soon allow your admittance."

"We are to blend in and walk in with them?" Mother Anne's sharp tongue pricked Father O'Brien. The black habits behind her all glared at the suggestion. Father O'Brien smiled. He turned toward the guard, "Harrison, see they come in with the women."

Proud to be addressed by his Christian name, Harrison snapped to attention. "I will, Father."

Just then an overwrought body slammed herself against the gate. She slid out of her coat as someone grabbed it, and she crumpled to the ground in her nightgown, pulling hunks of hair from her scalp. "My only child," she repeated, pressing her back against the steel gate. Mother Anne sat down next to the woman and wrapped her in her arms. The sisters spread among the people and tended those who waited outside Hell's gate.

Father O'Brien walked back into the courtyard and knelt down beside a dead man. He closed the man's eyes, "May you find peace in heaven." Then he moved on. The next victim looked like a teenager. His fleshless bone's held rosary beads untouched by flames. Blessing him, the priest scooped up ashes and made the sign of the cross on the young man's forehead and moved on.

The next corpse had a tiny cross pinned on the bill of his gray prison cap. Father performed the Office of the Dying. On and on, throughout the night Father O'Brien wandered among the carcasses, while the wind played with the black, thick smoke pushing it up and down on the prison yard and shooting flames out of barred windows while the bird-caged men coughed, burned and died. The Grim Reaper spread death's odor over the prison. It permeated rescuers' noses in a burnt flesh odor that would stay in their noses a lifetime. Hardened criminals loosed in the yard cried like babies when flames drove them further away from the men they were trying to rescue.

Around four in the morning, a fireman handed Father O'Brien a cup of coffee. "Let's sit on the chapel steps." He held the priest's elbow and led the way across the cadavers through ankle-deep water to Saint Catherine of Sienna Chapel where a few resting men gave up their places on the steps.

"God's-House-Behind-Walls." The fireman concluded. "I never thought I'd find myself here."

Father O'Brien blew on his coffee. "Eighty-five men received Holy Communion at Easter Vigil." He smiled warmly into the fireman's soot-circled eyes. The fireman looked back at the tired priest. "I walked among rows of dead men, many scarcely more than boys. May their souls rest with the Lord. They have been through Hell here on earth."

A convict yelled, "Hey, Father, over here!" The exhausted priest took a sip of coffee and stretched his aching legs then offered the fireman his hand.

"What is your name, son?"

"McWhorter, Christopher McWhorter."

Father O'Brien shook the man's hand and slipped into his native tongue, "Dian do Bheath, Christopher McWhorter. God bless your life."

CHAPTER 19: BLACK SMOKE AND BURNT LUNGS

Black smoke shadowed the walls of the atrium. Inching upward, it filled the lungs of men on Theo's tier. The acrid smoke singed off Theo's eyebrows and eyelashes deposing soot in his nose until his breathing became labored. Sweat flowed down his face and mixed with uninvited tears. Rescuers became blind before the impassable heat drove them back.

The smoke carried men's coughing, cursing and gagging, jagged screams until lungs burnt black flickered and went out as caged men died. Many men died with mouths open in a silent scream. Smoke and gases grew death faster than weeds in a freshly hoed row. Theo closed his eyes on the sight of himself brooding over his hoed row of corn at O.S.S.O. farm where thin, green weeds peeked at him, he thought as they sprouted at the beginning of the row he just hoed. He smiled.

Around him men's skin cracked open releasing blood with wisps of steam. As a beheaded chicken flaps its wings and flies around the barnyard, already dead, men made frantic, flapping sounds. Theo listened to his radio. "WAIU, we now break in with news of fire at the Penitentiary. Thank you, Lewis."

"Fire is believed to have started in Section I and is now licking the dry timbers of Section H. The fire has swallowed Section G. Listen as the men behind me yell to be let out of their locked cells." Every parent listening, who addressed mail to Sections I, H, and G were praying.

"We have been notified that burnt prisoners were evacuated to the basement infirmary to make beds available for those who have a chance to live. Now corpses are being brought back upstairs and laid in the courtyard. No reporters are allowed inside."

Theo found peace in knowing his son died sweetly rocking in his arms. "I am not afraid to die. My only wish is to be buried next to my son." He tilted his head back so he could see Holl.

"I bet you will be buried with him." Holl walked away from the barred window. He laughed sarcastically, "Son-of-a-bitch. I've been here thirty minutes. Would you say my luck ran out?"

"What can you expect, Holl? You should have known your cellblock was built over the penitentiary's previous cemetery. Didn't you know that? We are all going to melt down into the graves already beneath us." Theo remained on his mattress.

Holl spun around. "That ain't funny, Theo."

"But it is a fact."

"You are full of shit."

"Listen." Theophilus turned up his radio. "The Good Reverend is broadcasting from WAIU studio inside the prison walls." Sure enough, Reverend Wright was the voice on the radio telling about the cemetery beneath the Penitentiary.

Jimmy Henderson-Montgomery County, yelled, "Theo is full of shit, Holl. Reverend Wright never told the truth in his life or in the pulpit. The good Reverend is serving time for a double murder. Some say it is for killing two mistresses. Anyway he cannot see what is going on. His shit studio has no windows."

Holl exhaled. He pulled his gaze from Jimmy and searched Theo's face. "That true?"

Theo coughed at length. Prison etiquette, Don't butt in conversations! Worse, Holl knew the violation and still brought Jimmy into the conversation. "Decide yourself. It don't matter. Nobody is coming for us."

"You think so?"

Holl grabbed the radio. Lifted it over his head and slammed it on the concrete floor. The wood splintered freeing broken glass tubes across the cell. One unbroken tube rolled up against the leg of Theo's bunk.

"Hey, who turned off Firestone's Cavalcade of Death?"

Theophilus rolled out of the bed to the floor. His coughing did not stop. Thick smoke floated an inch above his nose. He opened his eyes and turned his head. Unconscious men lay in different angles of death across the tier. No longer did the dead feel their burning flesh. To his left, the cell housed moonshiners. "Let's drink to Prohibition, Theo." They used to tell him, waving every kind of fruit they sneaked out of the kitchen. Theo refused to drink the fermented fruit, knowing later that night the boys would deliver their hangover headaches to the toilet. From the punch bowl to the toilet bowl was their modus operandi. Theo could see the men kneeling with their heads in toilet water and their backs soaked with wet towels, dead they were.

An explosion super heated gas and knocked Holl down. He moved up on his knees. "God, I am unworthy, but only say the word . . ." Theo's eyes burned. He felt Holl's dead body next to him and he heard the sound of metal hitting locks as rescuers axed off locks and fingers on the tier below.

"Company K, marching through, Boss. Company K on the tier, Boss." Theo listened. Thousands of convicts huddled in the courtyard and it took Company K, the tough guys, the crazies to keep working on. They would be the ones to grab axes and separate locks. Company K the men with balls. The incorrigibles, bad asses, troublemakers. Company K was cloistered from the general prison population. Men in there had cut off their mother's tits, then killed them. There were men who rid their fathers of their seed by castrating them alive. The Cavalry. Theo crawled back up on his bunk. As a dead deer lies beside the road with his neck extended back in a final capture of air, so Theo arched on his bunk.

CHAPTER 20: WAIU, REVEREND WRIGHT

America finished supper gathered around the radio. Fathers propped their stocking feet up on ottomans, mothers took the darning egg out of their sewing baskets. Children sprawled on the floor for Firestone Hour.

"We interrupt this broadcast for a news flash from WAIU. I am Reverend Wright."

In West Jefferson, Ohio, George Albright ordered his children to bed. Their mother, Irene, followed the children down the hall, listened to their prayers and tucked them in. Returning to the living room she found George standing at the radio, staring at the small circle of glass over the dial numbers. "CBS has hooked up to WAIU. They are broadcasting directly from the pen."

Irene sat in her chair. She wanted George to sit also.

"Seventy-two stations have joined us here at CBS." George drove his fist into the top of the floor standing radio at the announcer's revelation. "The Ohio State Penitentiary is on fire and the prison campus is covered with men who have passed on."

"That sonofabitch, Irene. That Wright guy is calling it a campus. What the hell is going on?"

Irene walked over to George, "Come sit in your chair." They stared at the radio, unmoving and barely breathing.

"I can't." George paced angrily. Reverend Wright continued.

"The Red Cross is serving steaming hot coffee and meat sandwiches from its canteen."

"Damn. It is not a picnic." Irene placed herself between George and the radio. He might hurl it out the window like he did last fall when the Philadelphia Athletics began their 'Mack Attack' on George's hometown team, the Chicago Cubs. George was proud when it was announced the World Series would hold the initial game at Wrigley Field. He had high hopes until Connie Mack's team pounded them with the Mack Attack, in the fifth game. George heaved the radio out the window. When Irene returned from shopping she set her basket on the table and saw it lacked a radio. She did not ask about the game. She did buy a Motorola floor model, as insurance against the next time.

"The morale of the men is excellent," continued Reverend Wright.

"That is enough." George shoved Irene aside and unplugged the radio. The only sound in the room was George's angry panting. He put his head in his hands, sat down on the floor and sobbed. His entire body shook. The day George Junior was arrested for prohibition violations, George and Irene Albright told their younger children their brother enlisted in the army and would be gone for awhile.

~ ~ ~ ~ ~ ~

Rick Lemasters, studio manager of Columbia Broadcasting System, read his line, "I would like to thank all the people scheduled for programs for giving up their own programs. They willingly gave up their allotted time to allow the prisoner's names to be continued." Then sent the broadcast back within the prison where Reverend Wright was being fed names of victims on scraps of paper that littered the top of his studio desk until the wood was obliterated. Hundreds of tiny scraps of paper held names announced as fatalities, then withdrawn, some then amended bringing dead men back to life for the listeners' ears. And in the confusion, placed back into the fatalities wrenching listeners' hearts.

Party lines across America jammed. Prison telephone lines coiled into ashes. Reverend Wright continued on, "Prisoners and rescuers wade in ankle-deep water through a river of dead bodies. Hundreds of men move in the ghoulish scene, while injured men fear drowning in the watery lawn. They grab out at passing legs." Carried away with himself he described a prisoner, "The man slipped and fell between two charred bodies, landing face-to-face against a man whose nose was burned away and his lips curled like a potato chip that bends in boiling oil, the dead man grins."

Thousands of citizens clamored to the fire. Automobiles jammed the streets and Columbus policemen dotted the outside wall. National Guard troops ordered to storm the street with fixed bayonets marched up Spring Street and rounded the corner. They traveled Dennison, Maple and Dublin Avenue. Bedlam was dispersed for a short time.

A sub-machine gun brought from the guard's room was placed at the front gate. Thousands of milling prisoners were called but refused to assemble in the dining room. Like earthquake victims, the prisoners feared being inside a building. No one closed their eyes to sleep that night. Men kept vigilant for hot spots. Martial law was declared by the Governor, from the Allegheny Mountains where he was playing golf on the greens of Greenbrier Resort.

"It looks like only the dead will sleep tonight." The Reverend signed off.

~ ~ ~ ~ ~ ~

Five hours after the fire was knocked down, prisoners remained outside. The scene of confusion did not fade in the rising sun. Sunlight failed in the job the beacon lights and arc lamps had done on the arena. Prisoners still stood single file along the walkway of the Records Office. Overfilled gutters dripped water down on men, but no one cared.

"Hear Ye, Hear Ye, Step right up and get your yellow telegraph blank." A Trustee waved papers over his head. "Write a message to your family. We will send them your wire."

John Burden, Red Cross volunteer, stared back at the eyes of the unmoving man in front of him. He walked the length of the line giving the men the papers. The men stood idle. The handed papers dangled at their sides. He returned to the head of the line and asked. "Why didn't they move?"

"No pencils." Someone whispered from the queue of men.

Burden slapped his forehead. "Of course." He hollered for a Trustee to bring pencils. With that he left the men and went to gather more blank telegraph papers. When he returned the row of men had not moved. Now the lead men had papers in one hand and yellow pencils in the other and still they stared at him. He was puzzled.

"Many cannot write. Many have no idea where their families have moved." Burden turned to a tall woman with dark chocolate eyes and marcel waves in her hair. The Warden's daughter smiled confidently at him. Vivian Jackson was always on target. She was calm and collected. She ordered Trustees the same way she ordered the medical people with her 'carry-on' manner. The initial calls for medical people and clergy was her decision. Wherever she appeared, she knew exactly what the situation needed. She posted guards and removed prisoner-hating guards from the scene. She ordered the back gates unlocked when she saw a fire engine waiting. She stepped past Burden to the head of the line and he watched.

"Miss Vivian." The dazed man at the head of the line bowed.

"Hello, Kenneth."

Kenneth handed her his paper and pencil with the aplomb a kindergartner hands his first assignment to his teacher. Vivian beamed at him. "Come over here, Kenneth, and we will do your work at this table." Calmly she took the items from him. Kenneth followed. "Shall I tell them you are safe?" Kenneth nodded.

Burden watched the poised woman. Seeing the error of his ways, he asked three idle army men to step to Vivian's table. He turned and called up the next man in line. "This nice man will take care of you." The prisoner stepped up, only too proud to give his orders. Burden called the next two men to the waiting soldiers.

The natural born military man proudly took matters in hand. " What is your name?"

"Crit."

"Crit?"

"Yes. My pappy told Mama I looked like a little critter when I came out. It stuck! They gave me another name that Mama wrote in the Bible, but it's been so long, I forgot."

"Crit escaped."

"Oh hell, now they'll think I am on the run."

~ ~ ~ ~ ~ ~

At the Warden's residence, Prisoner Detail removed tables, chairs and bed. They loaded the house goods on trucks ready at the back gate where two shotgun ready guards oversaw the operation. Valuable mirrors and vanities were loaded very gently, Tiffany lamps and Arabian carpets. Prison trucks stood ready but the fire never threatened the area.

CHAPTER 21: HORTICULTURAL BUILDING

I gave the mob a long steady stare. Fear filled my steps. I waited. A spot opened and I stepped into the vacancy. Like a seamstress sews a fine seam, I threaded my way through a boisterous human fabric. People gathered in their own puddles of their own making. Anger, guilt and deep sadness pooled the sidewalk. Cautiously, I choose places to squeeze my frame and insert my body through the mob, twisting and turning my shoulders. I needled my way through the crowd avoiding angry, hate-filled men and sidestepping crazed weeping women. I directed my eyes down and sewed my way through. The belief the world had just broken open followed me as surely as thread follows a needle. The world shattered and Humpty Dumpty could never be whole again for these people. They will be the walking wounded. I walked closer to the curb embroidering a hem of safety between the uniformed black cap drivers of twenty shiny hearses freckled along the sidewalk's edge. Briskly I passed them.

At the Horticultural Building, I handed over a pencil-scribbled pass to a disinterested National Guard. He gave the note a cursory glance, once down then back up. He reminded me of a kid playing soldier and his unshaven youth bothered me. I've come too far to deal with his apathetic attitude. He opened the door and motioned me in. Then he stepped in behind me and shut the door on the riotous shouts behind us. "Wait here."

I released my tightly held breath, wondering how long I had not breathed. Toe-to-heel, the baby-face executed an about-face and marched over to confer with his hard-looking superior. The superior officer represented a long military life that gave him a hardness that men his age lack. His tanned, leather-looking skin gave him a war-likeness that was all about duty. Rifle and bayonet upward, he stared at me with deep-set eyes hidden under a cleft forehead. The toy soldier babbled on. When the kid stopped, the officer motioned for me to approach. The unforgiving concrete floor echoed my footfalls until I adopted a tiptoe fashion of steps.

"Ma'am." The officer dipped his chin and opened the door he was guarding. The unheated exhibition hall lay behind the door. The officer followed behind. I stood inside the room and looked at the tables cloistered around a group of empty wooden folding chairs. From the ceiling, on all four walls, hung alternating flags and black-draped crepe. "Have a seat, Ma'am."

A path divided the rows of unoccupied chairs, and I chose an end chair half way up the aisle. The straight back chair moaned under my weight, and I promised the chair not to be there any longer than necessary. The leather-skinned officer withdrew.

Drawing in a deep breath of memory, I scanned the room. Last summer's flowers filled this room during the Ohio State Fair last I was here. The glory of those colors and their sweet smell permeated this hall. These tables were a paradise of competing flower arrangements. Today, the concrete walls hold back the aroma in my memory.

Bang! I jerked. Double metal doors thundered in my ears. Flung open, the doors slammed against the walls. An olive-drab Army truck that previously transported men to the War-To-End-All-Wars arrived. Duty-of-the-day was transporting cadavers to this make-shift morgue. The Dance of Death began in a discorded symphony of grinding brakes, reverberating metal doors and keening unoiled Gurney wheels. Trucks arrived in the staccato of ants approaching a picnic and departed in a postlude of squeaking clutches and grating gears. The notes are played in a twenty-minute reiteration. Never varied, the trucks arrived pushing the cadent noise deeper and deeper into my brain until a migraine detonated. My icy fingers fumbled in an attempt to open my pocketbook. I lifted the bag and bit it open. Where are my Bayer? I rifled through the contents. Found! I scanned the room for a drinking fountain, and my eyes halted on a man standing just inside the door. He wore a badge and he stared at me through thick glasses which enlarged his eyes with pity. I looked away and swallowed the aspirin, sans water. I do not want pity.

Overhead, a ceiling of gridlock steel beams and a spider web of wires formed a maze over the room. There were pastel-painted pipes that meant something to somebody, somewhere, I supposed. I counted the network of wires and tried to block the noise from the work taking place around me. I never gained control of my jerking to the sounds of the trucks and the muffled thud of a hard, wrapped corpse hitting a table. The sound unhinged me and I fought for composure. Toe-tags have replaced last summer's ribbons of second place red, third place white and first place blue.

Gone are the brightly costumed vendors who welcomed visitors from all corners of the world. I met Canadians, people from the Far East and Europe. Now two-hundred National Guardsmen keep out the unwelcome.

Two women, reminding me of Carolina Wrens, shuffle up the aisle in nut-brown coats that are thread-worn from too many ammonia washes. Each woman is covered by a large nutmeg-colored scarf tied beneath her chin. The folded points of the cloth flap like tail feathers behind each nestling's head. The women hold hands. The smaller one's face is a half smile of indecision. She is not sure she should greet the people filing in and filling up the chairs, in the manner she greets church people. The stout one walks with lips sealed in a straight line of determination to get about their business.

The two women stop at the row in front of me, and the tiny one enters. She takes the third seat and leaves the larger bird to drop on the aisle chair. The tiny one has two full inches to spare on her chair seat. The stout one's backside droops over the sides of her chair. The wrens turn inward on each other, remove their scarves in mirrored reflection then stuff their scarves deep into their coat pockets. They turn sideways until their knees meet then turn their faces to me. "We were nearing our farm on National Road when our old nag picked up speed. She smelled her barn. Sheriff Porter rode up on us so fast he stopped in his own dust."

Stealing the story, the tiny one reported, "Removing his black ten gallon hat, he said, 'Sisters, get on over to the Penitentiary'." She fluttered and put her fingers over her mouth.

The stout woman shifted her heavy bulk and took back the story. "I am her sister. We are dear Walter's sisters. We live in Donnelsville. Sheriff Porter got off his horse and guided our weary-footed nag into a reluctant turn all the while she struggled against him and would have bit him, if she could have reached him."

The other bird cut in with the preciseness of a little girl cutting out paper-dolls. Never did they cut off the line and into a sister mid sentence. "Dear Walter's breath gets away from him. Sends him into terrible spasms." She drew her finger in a straight line across her throat. "His face turns blue and a coughing jag sets in on him. Prohibition Agents came up in the yard one night and asked for direction to Mrs. Corday's. Dear Albert provided them the way. Mrs. Corday runs a boarding house for girls who have violated the laws of chastity, so to speak. Well Agent King asked for a drink of water, and Dear Walter took him in the house to use the pump at our dry sink. When the Agent walked back through our parlor he spied dear Walter's Mason jar of gin by Walter's rocker rung. They took him off and we never saw him again."

"He got thirty days, Possession of Alcohol. Yep, that's what they can do and did."

A soldier leaned over a table, twisted a toe tag and called, "Walter Baily." He dropped the tag back against an exposed charred foot. The wren sisters inhaled and helped each other stand. A soldier came to their side and offered his elbows. I watched them slip their brown, age-spotted hands through his bent elbows. Their heads bobbed, they were ready. The soldier stepped out in half-stride, a falcon between two Carolina wrens whose spines had been bent by Life's burdens.

~ ~ ~ ~ ~ ~

A Fort Hayes Sergeant propped open the door and a thin stream of people entered taking seats in a polka dot pattern, leaving a lot of space between the dots. It built invisible walls of privacy among the occupants. A lone woman, painted by a wide black brush fixed her eyes on me and moved up the aisle under her wide-brimmed ebony hat, never breaking her stare. Her midnight dress ended just below her knees, flapper style and her black-hosed legs ended in Brunswick black shoes. She reminded me of a scissor cut silhouette. She stationed herself at my aisle. I moved my knees for her entry. She said, "I'm from Coshocton County. Here to claim my husband, Tom Holland. People call him Holl." She dropped off her words and moved on down to the other end of my row.

Now, my grandmother would say the lady 'unbossomed herself' in the way people did at train and bus stations. It was their way of filling uneasy dead air between them and a stranger. They state where they are from and why they are there to strangers who do not care nor want to know.

Suddenly, the flow of people at the door became clotted by a woman who was standing her ground. She was in a rant with the baby-face toy soldier who patiently waited for her tirade to run its course.

"Your son and husband's names are not on my list, Mam."

"The prison phoned and said they were." Her face shone with tears.

"The prison has no phone lines. You would have received a telegram." The woman held no faith in the soldier and she refused to move. Her blood-shot eyes rested on the soldier. Foamy spittle slipped from the side of her mouth and down her face, unfelt. She did not move. "His name again?' He looked at his clipboard.

"Schmitz with a 'z' not an 's'. And there is no 'd'."

The Guard rechecked his list. "You probably should go over to the Records Office." She was a broken spirit. She turned slowly and worked her way back up the line of people. Hungry and weak, she had gone without lunch because she lacked money for a meal and bus fare home. She hailed a cab and got in.

The cabbie started, "Last night I was in my cab listening to the broadcaster tell of a convict running out into the yard with his back on fire. He fell on the ground and a rat jumped out of his pocket. Isn't that funny? Convicts make rats pets and train them to bite. They sic them on people, like I do my dog. I took a convict once to the train station and he said his ears had been chewed off by rats."

"Shut up!" Mrs. Schmitz screamed.

"Ok." He glanced up at his rear view mirror. "I know it was awful the guards refused to give up the keys, change of shift and all. No one wanted to take on the responsibility. You know, what if it was false alarm, what if prisoners escaped?" He stopped the cab. For her, she left his question unanswered and left no tip. For him, he opened no door.

Mrs. Schmitz stepped out of the cab into the horrible smell of burnt flesh. It coated her tongue. Tiny molecules of unsettled black smoke lingered from the fire and turned her coat and pocketbook a dusky color. It coated her hair. Mother Anne's schoolboy Harrison had grown into his command over the three days. He met Mrs. Schmitz at the gate with well-founded confidence. "I must go to the Records Office." Her voice cracked. Because of the empathy Harrison had for all the people coming to claim their loved ones, he stepped up to her and went against regulations by taking her elbow. He gave her a warm smile.

"This man will take you." He motioned a man who came to Mrs. Schmitz with a caring air about him. "Be not afraid." He offered his arm. She stared at prisoners in the yard and the gun-mounted walls. The worst fear she had ever known filled her. "You will be safe." She took his arm. "I'm sorry about the water, but it had no place to go. The lawn was saturated."

She did not feel the coldness of the ankle-deep water. She watched the armed guards aligned on the top of the prison walls. Policemen milled around the yard. Sweat formed in her armpits and ran down her sleeves. She didn't know why she was so hot. Her body shook and she leaked unstoppable tears.

"It is only a short way now. We are going to that red brick building ahead." Her escort pointed. She tried to smile at the closeness of the building, but her lips stuck on her mouth in a pained grimace. The man took his time, thinking if he rushed her she would feel a sense of urgency in a dangerous situation and so he strolled. She kept focused on the building, and he felt some tension leave her body. "You know if my mother was here, I would want someone to walk her. I am very sorry for your circumstances, Ma'am, but I am glad I could help." She heard him but she could not take her eyes off her destination.

"It is a good sign. Them sending you to Records.

Many things happened last night." He kept up his chatter. "One man ran out safe and sound. He stopped and bent over to catch his breath and a kitten jumped from his pocket. The little fur ball sat down panting, his little tongue lopped out of the corner of her mouth. The guy looked at the kitten and said, 'Hey, I did all the running.' The man patted Mrs. Schmitz hand. "So you see if a little kitten made it, your husband probably made it also."

Her head turned and her eyes flashed. "I have a son and a husband here."

"I am sorry." He hoped she did not have a double loss. "I would just like for you to keep in mind, names and numbers don't mean anything today. In the panic of the night I knew a man rescuing men, his shirt got soaked from the spray of the fire hoses and another man handed him a dry shirt. The rescuer had a heart attack in the stair well. I tell you this not to upset you, but the coroner noted the stenciled number of the man's shirt and reported the name that went with the number, deceased."

Mrs. Schmitz stopped walking and turned to the man at her side. "How awful."

"Yes. The owner of the shirt met his wife who had been told to report to the Horticultural Building."

"What a shock that must have been for her."

"It was. So you see, try not to get all worked up. They have a lot of paperwork to straighten out." His warm eyes reassured her.

"Maybe you are right." She shook his hand.

"Good Luck."

She turned her back and climbed the steps where an unsmiling guard stood at the Records Office door glaring down upon her escort. She entered the building chiding herself for not asking her chaperon's name.

Outside at the bottom of the steps, Trustee 12721 prayed the best awaited the lady.

OHIO DOES BIT

At the direction of Governor Cooper, the Emergency Board has made provision whereby the victims of the fire at Ohio Penitentiary not only will be prepared for burial, but coffins and robes supplied and transportation provided for the bodies to their homes.

All arrangements have been completed enabling the bodies to be released to relatives or friends tomorrow morning. Burial and shipping permits have been provided, that relatives and friends may call at the temporary morgue on the State Fair Grounds, or wire instructions to the Warden at the penitentiary.

—*Enquirer Bureau Special Dispatch*
April 22, 1930, Columbus, Ohio

CHAPTER 23: *COLUMBUS CITIZEN* AD

Regardless of conclusion

of investigation,

families have no legal

recourse against

the State of Ohio and

can not sue for damages.

—Full page ad that appeared in *Columbus Citizen*, p. 17, April 23, 1930, Columbus, Ohio, addressing the State of Ohio's responsibilities regarding the fire

CHAPTER 24: REAL ACCOUNTS

I fought in the Argonne and St. Mihiel in France in the World War, and in all my foreign service never saw anything on the battlefield or in temporary hospitals to compare with the horrors in the prison yard during the prison fire.

—Captain Tom W. Jones, Middleport,
Legislative Representative, Meigs County, Ohio
Columbus Citizen, April 22, 1930

***

Nearly five thousand men were crowded inside an institution originally constructed for the safe keeping of 2,000, part of it so old that confederate officers captured during the Civil War were confined there.

—*Toledo Blade*

***

One inmate, unable to escape scrawled a simple note before he died of suffocation:

"Gus Socka. Notify John Dee, 93 Armory Av. Cincinnati."

***

JUST LEFT TO DIE

Cincinnati Prisoner Tells of Pleas - - - - Curse Guard's Reply, *Columbus Bureau*, 207 Spahr Building

Columbus, Ohio, April 21 — Albert Johnson, Cincinnati, a husky man well over six feet tall, wept as he showed his burned hands and told of the panic in the cells. "Mister, we pleaded and pleaded with that guard to let us out, but he wouldn't. He forced us back and then he ran out and we were left to die. When the firemen came they began to smash the locks. They's the way a few of us got out.

One man, Tucker carried six other men out to the open before he fell. Here is Tucker lying under this blanket."

***

COLUMBUS, O., April 22 (AP) — Two companies of regular Army troops and 1,500 Ohio National guardsmen were stationed at strategic places about the penitentiary.

Every guard on both day and night shifts was on duty. Beacon lights arc lamps placed upon the main wall for protection played down on the ghastly scene. Slowly the work of removing bodies proceeded.

***

They stood for hours around the main gate until each received the burial permit and went on to the fair grounds to claim the dead. Bertillon measurements, prison numbers and every other means of identification were checked to make certain there were no mistakes. Three men previously listed among the dead were reported today to be alive.

—Springfield Sun-Times
April 24, 1930

www.ingramcontent.com/pod-product-compliance
Lightning Source LLC
Chambersburg PA
CBHW072112170626
46813CB00004B/1510